The Copper Shakes

Books by Kee Briggs

The Third Removed
The Painted War
Finders-Keepers
Losers-Weepers
The Painted Lady
A Few Good Old Men

The Usher Orlop Mysteries
The Golden Janus
The Pewter Masks
The Nickel Trophy
The Bronze Bones
The Brass Portraits
The Zinc Ormolu
The Silver Scepter
The Rhodium Dragon
The Copper Shakes

The Asti Fantasies

Charm Catcher
Dream Weaver

Ebook

Write to Live Longer

The Copper Shakes

Kee Briggs

Keescapes Publishing
Satellite Beach, Florida

The Copper Shakes

Keescape Publishing books may be ordered through booksellers or by contacting:
Keescape Publishing
90 Flamingo Dr.
Satellite Beach, Florida 32937
www.keescapes.com
KeescapesPublishing@gmail.com

This is a work of fiction. All characters, names, incidents, organizations are all figments of the author's imagination and are used fictionally.

ISBN 978-0-9820044-4-9
Published in the United States of America

The Copper Shakes

Kee Briggs

CHAPTER 1

Usher was about a half an hour early, but that was perfectly all right. He needed to relax for a little bit. It had been a straight through drive from Denver to Albuquerque. Although he'd enjoyed stretching his classic 1965 Shelby Mustang, he needed to organize his thoughts for the business at hand before meeting his client's ex-wife. Although there had been no warning he might be stepping into an adversarial situation, Usher could see all the earmarks were present.

The client, Mark Hullscraper, was a hotshot executive for Kleenalot with headquarters in Chicago. What little Usher knew about him spoke of money. Because of the other clients that he had in the Chicago area, Usher recognized the home address as being in an upscale district. The $6,500 fee had been accepted without a gasp or comment. The only stipulation was that Usher not reveal the price to his ex-wife.

On the other hand, the ex-wife's house was in an older section of Albuquerque. The area had been developed when lots were figured in fractions of an acre instead of square feet.

Usher spotted the house number on the road side mailbox,

but the owner's car wasn't there yet. He didn't want to pull into the single car driveway, so he'd be hemmed in when the wife returned.

Usher pulled across the street into a driveway of an obviously vacant house with a "For Sale" sign on what used to be a lawn. He leaned back to change out of the driving position. He took a swig of cold coffee from a paper cup with a plastic top. The resulting shudder could have come from either too cold drive-through coffee or the plastic caps, neither were to his liking. While checking for the car again, Usher noticed a kid walking down the road in the direction from which he had come. When the figure drew closer, it turned out to be a boy in jeans and sneakers, wearing a school-boy style jacket and carrying a blue backpack.

When the kid reached the client's driveway, he squatted down to tie his shoe. While scrunched down, he continued to examine the house as he picked at the shoelace. He looked both ways before striding purposefully inside the rail fence and along the driveway to the house. Then he veered off into the remains of a substantial garden. After plucking off a couple of scubby tomatoes, he pulled a gnarled carrot from the ground. Loose dirt on the carrot was rubbed off on the pumpkin vines. After another quick check of his surroundings, the kid moved out of sight along the garage.

Usher made a quick survey of the property. The Hullscraper residence was a single-story dwelling. It was pretty much an island. To the right was a horse pasture. Vacant land ran off to the rear. On the left was the remains of a fireplace. The lot directly across the street was also barren. The nearest neighbor was where Usher was parked. There was a solid six-foot privacy fence enclosing the backyard. It encompassed a side yard before attaching to the front of the house. There were about 8 feet between the garage and the fence. Unless the kid belonged there and he had a key to the house, he'd be enclosed in the backyard.

Usher decided to wait to see what happened. About 20 minutes later, he noted a vehicle approaching. In case it was Mrs. Hullscraper, he stepped out of the car to the street. A well used tan van slowed to turn into the drive.

Trotting toward the van, Usher raised his hand. The vehicle stopped just before entering on the gravel drive.

The occupant was a woman. She rolled down the window a couple of inches.

"Mrs. Hullscraper, I am Usher Orlop."

"Oh, Mr. Orlop, I'm sorry I'm late." She rolled the window down further.

"Do you have a young boy wearing a blue jacket in your family?"

"No, there're just me and my daughter."

"The kid just picked something from your garden and disappeared around the garage. Is there another exit from the backyard?"

"No."

"If you watch the front, I'll go around and see what's happening. Honk if he comes out this way."

"Oh, that might be dangerous."

"He is not big enough to be of any great threat."

Usher stayed off of the noisy gravel and move through the garden patch to a point where he could see down the length of the garage. He was surprised to see that the garage was double the normal length.

He moved down the wall of the building to the back corner. Cautiously he peered around the edge.

About 18 feet away, a figure was leaning against the garage wall, fast asleep. His chin was on his chest. Both forearms were on the sparse grass.

Usher move closer. The carrot top and the tomato stems were in a little pile. There was a hose bib at the corner. The splash block was wet. He' taken a drink and probably washed his veggies. There is also a wet spot at the bottom of the fence where he had taken a leak.

Moving into a somewhat defensive stance, Usher used his left foot to tap the kid's sneaker. There was a little drowsy movement, then the eyes popped open. He glanced at Usher and quickly checked his surroundings. The boy made no attempt to stand, but insolently collected himself into a more erect position. When he looked up at Usher, a sneer slid across a very handsome young face. The right upper lip twitched as he demanded, "Why'd you wake me up?"

"A better question is, why are you here?"

"What's it to you. You own this dump?"

"No, this dump belongs to me," said Mrs. Hullscraper, who was leaning against the corner of the building. Looking up at Usher, she said, "What have we here?"

"It would appear that we have a surly runaway, who is older than he appears at first glance. He's been on the road a while from all the dirt and odor he's collected. And he has a poor attitude and a smart mouth."

Looking down at the kid, Usher said, "Is that about right?"

The kid started to rise but Usher stepped on his foot preventing any movement. "Just stay put until we decided what we're going to do."

"What's your name?" said Mrs. Hullscraper.

The kid remained silent. He let the smirk on his face say

"go to hell."

Usher briefly entertained the impulse to backhand the expression off the little smartass but in illumined self-interest, he said instead, "Call him anything... 'sweetness or honey buns'."

Mrs. Hullscraper snickered.

"I'm not going to be around this outhouse long enough to need a name."

"It seems as if you're the one making it an outhouse," said Usher as he nodded toward the wet fence.

"Get off my foot so I can go." The lip rolled up in a sneer. It appeared the kid was ambidextrous in the lip curling.

Usher glanced at Mrs. Hullscraper, who said, "Let him go. I was entertaining the thought of letting him shower and wash his clothes, but if he is bent on leaving this dump, I won't stop him. He's too rancid to keep around here."

There was only a moment's hesitation before he relaxed down into his prior sitting position. He wasn't about to actually accept the offer but he would allow the offer to be forced upon him.

"If he can get himself clean enough, to enter polite society again, I might even give him something to eat. Won't be fancy but it's what Lindee and I eat."

"Are you sure you want 'twitchy-lip' here in your house?" said Usher.

"There is a bathroom with a shower in my studio." She patted the wall that she was leaning against. Old stinky here wouldn't like climbing through the panties and bras in my bath.

"Name's 'Rube'."

"Well Rube, I didn't think you're going to be around here

long enough for us to need a name," said Usher.

All he got for his observation was a scowl and a lip twitch.

The house owner shoved herself away from the wall. "This way." She led the way into the backyard.

Usher motioned the kid to follow. The sculptor brought up the rear, thus getting a brief opportunity to look at the woman he'd dealt with over the phone.

She appeared to be in her late 30s, with what would probably be called dishwater-blond hair. There was something wrong with her gait. The heavy long jacket covered most everything else. She was wearing jeans and low-heeled cowboy-looking boots.

Usher switched his attention to his surroundings once they turned the corner into the backyard. The whole yard was enclosed by a solid 6 foot privacy fence. In addition, there was another fence which arced out into the yard. It was attached to the far back corner of the house and swept to about 6 feet from the rear fence.

The interesting part of the yard were all the concrete drain pipes planted into the ground. All had boards sitting on top. On a few of the boards were terra-cotta, ceramic houses.

"This is my studio," said Mrs. Brown. It's toasty warm in here. The kiln is cooling after a firing."

The studio is about the size of a double car garage. The two sliding glass doors and a passage door faced the yard. The owner unlocked the passage door and led the way inside. She pointed at the door straight ahead. "That's the shower. Just a moment." She opened the door on the right that went into the garage. She disappeared just long enough to grab the white laundry basket and a large, worn bath towel. She set the basket in the bathroom doorway. "There are bath towels on the rack above the toilet. When you get out of the shower you can either wrap yourself in this or I can lend you one of my daughter's pink bathrobes. Toss all your clothes into the basket along with any dirty things in your pack. Be sure to clean out your pockets. Toss in the sneakers and the pack too."

Rube stood slack-hipped and looked directly at Usher and his momentary benefactor. With a rolled lip sneer he said in his best "smartass" tone, "If you think it will do you any good to get all my clothes away from me so you can call the cops so they can send me back wherever I came from, forget it. I don't have any family. I've been in foster care all my life. When my caseworker found out I was gone, she started celebrating and is still doing so. The county isn't going to spend a nickel to get me back. Just let me go my own way and everyone will be happier."

"Don't worry, I'm not going to call anyone. I'm just an environmentalist doing my bit to reduce pollution. Shampoo twice."

There is a general shuffling in the bathroom. Both adults stood waiting to see which way this scenario was going to go.

As clothes were removed, they were chucked into the basket. Shoes, backpack and shorts came out last. A bare foot push the basket out of the doorway and the door shut. The lock snapped.

Mrs. Hulkscraper had a broad smile on her face as she turned her attention to Usher.

For his part, Usher was wearing a frown. "I don't know about letting that snarly little whelp into your house..."

"Oh, I have always had a soft spot for pound puppies."

The shower water went on.

"While we have a moment, let's get a little business out of the way. First, I'm Carlee Brown and my daughter is Lindee Brown. I went back to my maiden name."

"I'll bet you were relieved to get rid of that load. I answer better to Usher...to you, but to him we're Mrs. or Ms. Brown and Mr. Orlop. He needs to earn familiarity.

"Oh, I wholeheartedly agree. Next, here are my car keys. Please bring my car into the garage and then you can park in the driveway."

"Right, I'll be back in a moment."

Carlee hit the button beside the entry door to the house and the garage door slipped up.

Quickly, Usher rounded up the cars. When he returned Carlee was in the kitchen.

"Are you a coffee drinker?"

"Real coffee."

"Good, I don't have any of that instant stuff in the house."

Usher paused to listen. He could hear the shower water over the gusher of water in the washer. The bathroom door was still closed.

"Come in. Have a seat. I have a problem to discuss with you." Carlee was indicating a small kitchen table with four straight back chairs. We can watch the studio from here."

As Usher seated himself, he said, What's our problem?"

Carlee set three mugs on the table and pulled out another chair. "This last weekend when Lindee and I were out in the woods collecting, Lindee found some poison ivy. At the moment she is all gooped up with calamine lotion. This morning she woke up with a fat lip and puffy eyes. I talked with the school nurse. The prognosis is that it will be a couple or 3 days before her face will be back to normal.

"I would have called you, but I knew you had already left. It's too expensive to make two trips and the cost of motels is going out of sight.

"So, I was thinking. My ex-husband and I used to do a lot of camping. He wanted a son and I gave him a daughter, but he forged ahead and tried to make a tomboy out of Lindee. We have good air mattresses and sleeping bags. If you'd like, you can stay here. I'm sorry for the delay."

Frequently, something spoils the best laid plans. I usually find a motel with a reasonably good restaurant and bar. I'd like to meet my subject and then I can find a motel. You're right, it's not a commuter drive."

Lindee will be a home from school pretty soon."

"Before she gets home, I like to find out a thing or two. Your husband...ex-husband, commissioned me to execute a silver mask of 'his daughter'. He made two specifications. The first is that I can not reveal the price I am charging to produce the mask."

Carlee laughed. "That sounds like that cheap, vindictive bastard. He's still ticked that I changed my name and Lindee's name back to Brown. Lindee is his proof to the world that he isn't gay. That's why he wants the mask...so he can say, 'Oh, look at my daughter'. He doesn't want me to know how much you're charging him because he is so far behind in the support payments that I might refuse to let you make the mask and demand that money be sent to me. What was the other provision?"

"He sent $1000 that I am supposed to give to you once I have satisfactorily completed my work."

"Ha! I told you he was a bastard. He knows the house taxes are coming up soon and I'll need that and more, but

$1000 would really help. To get that money, he knows I can't stand in your way.

Usher nodded in the direction of the studio. "You have anything of value out there?"

"Nothing of pawn value that a kid can carry off." Carlee watched Rube with a towel wrapped around his waist, slowly paddle about the studio in a thorough, systematic inspection.

"Have you ever seen such a perfectly proportioned and handsome young male before?"

Usher didn't answer for a bit. "I guess I haven't but I have a hard time getting past that sneer. I've dealt with a lot of kids. I found that the truly beautiful ones aren't always the best looking."

"Oh, I'll agree with that, but what bothers me now is that kid has the all physical raw materials to take the world by storm. Look at that face, when he's not playacting. He could be the feature model for Pierre Cardin or Ralph Louran. Or he could be a parts model for any class product."

"You're right. However, if the inside can't be changed, the outside will just bring him trouble."

Rube passed out of view behind the bath. "May I use your studio when I pull the mold?"

Certainly, what do you need?

"Not much. I need a table for Lindee to lie on. She should wear something without a collar. I need a plug-in and a water source."

"The studio has all that."

"Oh yes, I need you present."

"Oh good, I'll be able to watch. Incidentally, if next week I were to call you to ask you to drive down here to make a mask of Rube, what would you charge?"

"$6500."

Both Usher and Carlee grinned.

To get to another subject, Usher asked, "What kind of a potter are you? I see the wheel out there but I don't see much evidence of throwing."

"I used to, but I have scoliosis. I can no longer bend over a wheel hour after hour. I don't have the arm strength anymore. I started making clay models of adobe houses. That's why I have all those stands in the backyard. The models look great out in the yard, in plantings and natural settings."But they're very hard to make. The breakage and warp rate is quite high."

"What's that tall one with the crooked roof?"

Carlee laughed, "Oh, those are my favorites, but I can't do them commercially. The breakage rate is far too high. I once came across a magazine on Faeries. The imagery really fascinated me. I subscribe to the magazine. I still play around with them, but I never solved the roof problem."

"I wish you luck. Those are enchanting."

"At the moment, I'm working on another line. It is front walls of a city as you might expect to encounter on Barsoom, Edgar Rice Burroughs Martian cities or in Conan's time. There is an example on the far wall of the living room."

Usher went to take a look at the relief as Carlee poured the coffee. She stuck her head into the garage to yell at her puppy dog. "Rube. You drink coffee?"

"Got milk?"

"Little or lots?"

"Lots."

Carlee sloshing some coffee into a mug and drowned it in milk. She went out to the laundry. "Your coffee's here," she yelled as she begins shifting clothes into the dryer.

Rube retrieved his coffee from the shelf where Carlee had set it. He grunted and went through the door into the backyard.

Usher returned to his spot at the table in time to watch the tenderfoot advance across the gravel to the Faerie house. When Carlee finished with the laundry transfer, Usher nodded toward the yard. "Looks as if your work has another admirer." Rube was minutely inspecting it. At that moment, the kid happened to glance toward the house and spotted the watchers. He immediately draped a scowl over his face and turned away with a role of shoulders designed to show worthlessness or disdain.

"Arrogant little whelp," said Usher.

"Oh, he's just playacting. He hasn't let us see the real kid yet."

At that moment, a tornado hit the front door. It slammed as a backpack hit the floor simultaneously with a hearty yell, "I'm home." By the time the two words were uttered a little pixie skipped across the living room until she could see the man sitting at the table. "Is this Mr. Orlop?" Suddenly, the tornado came to a dead stop when she spotted a half-naked boy in her backyard.

"Who's that?"

"Oh, just a stray I picked up this afternoon."

"Oh, Moooooom."

"Say hello to Mr. Orlop and let him look at the mess you have sitting on your shoulders."

"Hi Mr. Orlop, I'm Lindee. I'm sorry I wasn't more careful where I went. I'm a mess. I've been trying not to scratch."

"It's just a temporary problem," said Usher to ease the situation.

Carlee had poured a glass of milk and fished two granola bars out-of-the-box. "Go out and introduce yourself to the boy and give him a bar. He snarls but I don't think he bites."Without any hesitation, Lindee took a slurp out of the glass, grab the bars and headed for the backyard.

Both Usher and Carlee were attuned to the impending meeting of the two diametrically opposed personalities. Carlee cringed as the half-glass studio door banged. "You always know where Lindee is. She lives in a nest of noise."

As soon as the door started to open, Rube became alert. Usher expected him to become self-conscious when confronted with a young girl, but he just dropped into an insolent slouch-hipped stand and waited.

"Hi, I'm Lindee. I'm having my afterschool snack. Mom sent this out." She tossed the bar into the air. Rube had to come out of his slouch to grab it.

"What's your name and where's your clothes?" Then she sat down on one of the concrete pipes and chomped off another chunk of granola.

"Rube."

"Hi Rube. Where's your clothes?"

"They're in the washer. I wasn't clean enough to suit your mother."

"Don't feel lonely. Nobody is. You're not from around here."

Rube sat on a pipe too, so he could use both hands to open the bar wrapper. His lurch to catch the bar had loosened the wrap around his waist. He had to set his coffee mug on the ground.

"How do you know?"

In a bell-like tinkle, Lindee laughed. "You've got all the color of a fish belly."

"You're in no position to say anything about color. Have you looked in the mirror lately."

Usher had been on half-full alert, waiting to see if any fireworks develop between the kids. They seem to hit a level where both were relaxed.

Turning his attention back to Carlee, he said, "Those cityscapes are great. I would expect a good reception in both the art and the decorator circles."

"Yeah, I can't build any backlog. My galleries keep dunning me for more. They're pretty labor intensive. I worked out most of the bugs now so I can keep warpage and cracking within acceptable limits."

"Just an observation...if you can't build an inventory, your prices are too low."

"They probably are. I have a hard time putting the right price on my things. Friends say that I don't value my talent enough."

Pricing is one of the areas where an artist needs to experiment as much as you do with your different clay bodies."

"When I settle on a design form, all I'll have to reshape my kiln. Now it's a top loader and I have to have Lindee help getting the green-ware in."

"Is Lindee going to be a potter?"

"Oh, definitely not. She doesn't like to get her hands dirty. She is much too feminine to wrestle in the dirt. And the arts are too lonely for her. She is a people person. Fortunately, as I get weaker, she is getting stronger and I still have enough clout to make her get her hands grimy."

"If Lindee is so important and her dad makes good money, why is he so far behind on his support payments?"

"Oh, it's not that he is overwhelmed with love for his daughter. As I said, she's a symbol."

Usher raised eyebrows.

When Mark and I met, he was a salesman. He could sell almost anything—vacuum cleaners, used cars, encyclopedias. It really didn't matter what he sold, he could make a living. After we married and had Lindee, he went looking for something with a higher earning potential.

"He went to work for Kleenalot selling industrial strength cleaners for all the cleaning needs of large commercial buildings. He worked his way into a good-sized territory in the Southwest.

"Mark and I used to work with a little community theater down the road. Mark was a good character actor. In one of the plays, he was a gay guy.

"One day when he was in Phoenix, he was leaving a large downtown office building and he stopped off at a public restroom. It was dirty. Just for fun, he came flouncing out of the restroom yelling in a high effeminate voice demanding to see management. He even threw a real hissy fit. He was dragging both male and female managers into the men's room to see the ring around the toilet.

"Anyway, just to shut him up, he got an order big enough to keep that whole building spotless for 10 years.

Usher was chuckling over the imagery portrayed.

"Mark finally found his calling. He has the largest territory in the company and it is the most lucrative. With such newfound fame and fortune, who needs an ailing wife and a daughter...when he really wanted a son?"

"So, why the mask?"

Mark has perfected his gay sales persona to the point that most everyone thinks he's gay. Before this whole thing started, he was actually launching some vicious barbs at homosexuals. He'll use the gay thing to make money but needs to be considered straight. He wants the mask as a proof he's not a poof."

Usher rolled his eyes.

Lindee came breezing into the kitchen, clunking her milk glass into the sink and started to walk away. Carlee pointed at the glass. Her daughter reversed directions. As she rinsed the milk out, she said, "Rube used to live on a ranch. He can't stand warm milk straight from the cow."

"You squeeze more information out of him than we did," said Usher.

"He's not as tough as he wants everyone to believe. He doesn't know much. He asked a bunch of dumb questions about pottery."

Outside, Rube had resumed his close inspection of all Carlee's work. Usher wondered how he could stay outside in just a towel with the chilly weather.

"They probably didn't have a pottery on the farm," said Carlee. Did you find out anything about his plans?"

"He's just passing through. He's headed for Cocoa Beach, Florida."

"What's he got? A thing for rockets?"

Lindee giggles. "No mom, he has heard that there were girls in bikinis all over the beaches and they're free."

"At his age?" said Carlee, as she looked accusingly at Usher.

Usher smiled. "He's not experienced enough to know that

'free' isn't usually free."

"Males," said Carlee in mock disdain.

Usher excused himself to use the bathroom. He headed for the one in the studio. In that utilitarian facility the only flat surface was the top of the toilet tank. Rube's worldly goods were laid out in a neat row. The commanding object was a Rubik's cube. Usher smiled. Everyone probably thought Rube was short for Rubin.

A few coins held down a small fold of bills. There wasn't much there. However, the most interesting thing was a small stack of 3 x 5 white file cards. The top card had an elaborate pencil drawing of what appeared to be a tribal symbol within an elaborate, complicated layout. It was well executed. Usher would have liked to see if there were any other drawings, but even though Rube was an arrogant, surly manifestation, those were his personal properties.

When the buzzer went off in the dryer, Carlee yelled at Rube. "Come get your toasty warm clothes."

Rube retreated to the bathroom to get dressed. Carlee went back to the kitchen to start dinner."I'll bet that kid has an iron will. He was turning blue staying in the yard. It's too late in the year to be outside practically naked as the sun dropped behind the building. He could have come into the studio at any time."

"It seems important to him not to show any sign of weakness."

Carlee banged a kettle down on the counter a little harder than necessary. "What a waste. You'll stay for dinner won't you? As I told our harlequin, it won't be fancy."

Usher would rather have found a decent bar and restaurant but as his eyes followed the freshly cleaned kid, who had just started investigating a great stack of magazines in a bookshelf, Usher wasn't sure that leaving him with a little slip of a girl and a disabled woman was a good idea.

"Thank you. I live a pretty solo life and I don't often have an opportunity to compare notes with other artists. Also, I deal with a lot of kids but only for less than an hour and then I'm a stranger putting them through strange things. I'm getting a kick out of Lindee's effervescence."

"Good. It's nice to have company. It helps to dilute Lindee's effervescence." Carlee put the pot with water on the stove.

Carlee chatted merrily as she dumped a couple of boxes of macaroni into the pot. While that was cooking, she cut up several little hot dog sized Polish sausages. The sausages and a box of frozen petite peas went into the pot when it had a couple of minutes to go.

Cabbage, carrots and onions went through the food processor to make slaw.

"Lindee, come make the dressing." True to her mother earlier statement, one could follow the daughter's progress through the house from the scrape of the chair that is being shoved away from the desk, the slam of the bedroom door to the hand slap on the hall door, where she paused long enough to give a short rendition of the beat to her current song of favor. Bare feet slaps on the tiles between the rugs charted her progress through the living room.

"You staying for dinner, Mr. Orlop?"

"Yes."

While Carlee drained the macaroni, Lindee started sloshing the ingredients, her mother had set out, into a bowl.

"I need to wash up," said Usher. "You want me to round up our foursome?"

"Please."

Rube was sitting on the cot curled into a "C" with his back against the wall and his heels on the edge. A magazine was held against his raised thighs.

"Dinner's ready."

Rube glanced up to acknowledge the announcement, but didn't offer any comment. Usher passed on into the bathroom. All of Rube's worldly goods had disappeared back into his pockets or pack.

When Usher emerged from the bath, Rube put down his magazine and lurched erect. The two males filed into the kitchen.

Lindee was setting the table and directing traffic. "Rube, you sit by the window." There was a bowl of coleslaw at each place. Carlee was serving plates from the pot.

Carlee distributed the plates and seated herself. "This restaurant won't take any prizes but this will hold you over until breakfast.

Usher was enjoying the aroma the Polish sausage provided and he found the fare very palatable. However, Rube was resting his left temple against his fist as he carefully extricated each pea out of the mac and cheese. He was herding them toward the edge of his plate.

"What's wrong with the peas?" demanded Lindee.

"Don't eat peas," came the sullen reply.

"Mom, he's not eating is peas and he's got his elbow on the table."

The elbow slowly came down, but he continued to shuffle peas. "Don't eat peas."

Carlee shrugged. "It'll just stunt his growth."

When Lindee started say something, her mother cut her off. "Don't even try. You need all the peas you can get."

Turning to Usher, Carlee said, "Tomorrow, after Lindee gets home, I'm going to open the kiln. This is an anxious time. I think I've settled on a formula to do those plaques. I'll find out tomorrow."

Rube had removed all the objectionable objects from his dinner. He was now eating with an intense single-mindedness that attracted the attention of the other diners.

"There is more in the pot," announced Carlee.

To keep everyone from watching Rube, Usher asked, "Are the new plaques similar to the one in the living room?

"The same dimensions but these are for entirely different scenes. I'm experimenting with different styles and subjects to see which attracts the most attention."

"I have a friend who has built the most fantastic facade in front of his house. Tanner Jones's driftwood forest..." There was an immediate reaction from Rube to Tanner's name.

"Do you know Tanner?" said Usher

Ruby slowly raised his eyes to look at Usher. "No." The kid dropped his gaze back to his plate and returned to eating.

Usher went on to describe Tanner and his creativity. "He has an old army truck on which he mounted dual front wheels so he could run on the sand. Have you ever seen the western beaches?"

"No."

"There are miles and miles of driftwood thrown up on the beaches. Tanner rigged an A-frame on the back of the truck for handling heavy objects. Whenever he finds a driftwood tree, he hauls it back to his place and plants it in front of the house. You can no longer see the house through the forest."

"Where is this enchanting forest?"

"South of Tillamook, Oregon. I think you'd enjoy Tanner. It seems to me that your creative bents lean in the same direction."

"Hey mom, if we can ever take a vacation, we can go up there and see it," said Lindee.

"We'll have to put it on a list. There are so many places I'd like to see."

While Rube was picking the peas out of a second helping of mac and cheese, Usher said, "Is Rube short for Rubik's?"

Rube continued to shove the peas about as he weighed the hazards of being truthful. Seeing no danger, he said, "Yeah."

"Oh, you know how to play the cube?" demanded an excited Lindee. "We have a kid in school, who is really good. He can do it in just over two minutes. He's working on getting his time under two."

Lindee's excited declaration netted her a first-class, rolled lip sneer and a depreciated grunt.

"Can you do better?"

"Lots better."

"Show me. Show me please," cried Lindee. "Do you have a cube with you?"

Rube gave an infinitesimal nod.

"Where? Can I go get it?"

"Hold on," said her mother. "If he has a cube, it's his and in his things, which are off-limits to you."

"Sorry," said Lindee.

Carlee left the table to take a carton of ice cream out of the freezer. "Let the poor guy finish dinner..

Rube it's getting too late to hit the road. If you want, you can have that cot in the studio tonight. It's not all that comfortable, but it's better than sleeping under a bridge and a heck of a lot warmer."

Rube nodded his acceptance.

Carlee collected the plates. She handed the one with the peas on it to Lindee saying, "Put these in the bird feeder."

"Okay." Lindee banged her way through the three doors to the backyard.

"Get my cube." said Rube as he left the table.

While the kids were gone, Usher said, If that offer of an air mattress still stands, I like to take you up on it."

"You're worried about Rube." That wasn't a question.

"He's too much of an unknown quantity and I'd hate to have something happen to my model before I get my mold."

Carlee laughed. "Yes, the offer is still open and thank you. Sometimes I don't think things out."

Both of the kids returned to the kitchen. Lindee had to rinse the plate. Rube's attention focused on the half gallon of chocolate, almond ice cream. It seemed as if he was trying to devour it with his eyes. He even forgot to sneer.

Lindee slid into her chair. Her eyes were glued to the cube in Rube's hand. After her mother's reprimand, she was hesitant to push for a demo. The meal wasn't over yet.

To refocus attention, Carlee said, "It'll be a bit before I can serve the ice cream. How about showing us how that thing works."

Rube handed it across the table to Lindee. "Mix it up."

Lindee's hands were so small she had difficulty grasping the cube and manipulating it. Although it was a struggle, she proceeded with steadfast determination until the cube was thoroughly jumbled.

By the time her arms were withdrawn from handing the cube to Rube, the cube's realignment was well along the way. Rube's hands were a blur.

"WOW!" yelled Lindee, expressing the unanimous opinion. "How fast was that?"

Rube shrugged. "I'm trying to get down under 30 seconds."

Usher smiled. Rube had forgotten to sneer.

"I want to time him. Who's got a secondhand?"

"I have a stopwatch on my Casio, said Usher. He began to change functions while Lindee mixed up the cube. Out of three more attempts, Rube's best time was 33 seconds.

Lindee was mightily impressed. "Can I take him to school with me tomorrow? I want to show him off?"

Carlee laughed as she started scooping ice cream into the bowls. "Of course not. Come right home after school. I want to unload the kiln and start another firing.

After finishing the ice cream, Carlee poured coffee for Usher and herself. "Lindee, have Rube help you get an air mattress and a sleeping bag down. Put Rube on the pump while you get two pillows, casings and a flannel sheet for Rube. That's all he'll need with the kiln. Then the two of you can do the dishes.

"Rube, you know how to do dishes, I presume?"

"Yeah, I know how to do dishes." The sneer returned. Usher and Carlee settled down in the living room. "I've been watching your pound puppy," said Usher. "I think you're right. He's playacting. That sneer slips every once in a while. Not much gets past him.

Carlee laughed. "I've been watching him watch you. I imagine he's trying to figure out who you are and why you're here."

"What are you going to do with him?"

"I'm just going to play it by ear. Either he'll just disappear or he'll open up and tell me a story. It may not be true, but it will be a starting point."

There was a general shuffling in the small glassed-in room off of the dining room. There was a raucous clatter as Rube threw his back into using a pump that was reminiscent of an old-fashioned tire pump.

After the bedding was arranged and the dishes done, Lindee had to go to her homework. Rube retreated to the cot where he resumed his systematic devouring of a great stack of ceramics and Faerie magazines.

CHAPTER 2

It was just beginning to get light when Usher awoke. As he opened his eyes, he was greeted with the unblinking stares of dozens of small, stuffed animals that line the edges of the room. Usher rolled over to inspect the menagerie on the other side of the room. When the day brightened, Usher retrieved his Elph digital camera that he carried in a case on his belt and took lower-level photos of his companions.

He could hear activity in the other end of the house, so Usher dressed and headed for the studio bathroom. Rube was still in bed, but Usher was sure he was feigning sleep. By the time of Usher came out, Rube was dressed and reading.

"Good morning."

Rube grunted a greeting.

A flurry of pink swept in from the bedroom wing. "Good

25

morning Mr. Orlop. Mom will be out as soon as she can smell the coffee." Lindee snapped the switch on the pot, sneaked a peek into the studio and was off again.

Usher hunted up a couple of mugs while he was waiting for the coffee. Rube took his turn in the bathroom and then braved the morning cold to go into the backyard and take another look at the Faerie houses.

Carlee arrived as Usher was pouring the coffee. She was wearing a long robe. Usher noticed that the hem on one side was closer to the floor than on the other. After small talk about the air mattress and the staring animals, Usher nodded toward Rube and repeated his question of the night before. "What are you going to do about him? If I wasn't here, you'd be alone with him as soon as Lindee leaves for school. He's not very big, but also you're not all that strong."

"I still have some time, so I'm just going to sit and wait." Carlee reached over and tapped on the window and held up her coffee mug. Rube acknowledged the offer and headed in. Carlee poured some coffee and lots of milk and then stuck the mug in the microwave to re-warm it.

Carlee sat for three sips of hot coffee before getting a pot of water going. When Rube came in he was in his stocking feet.

"Good morning Rube. Where are your shoes?"

Rube didn't return the greeting, but did explain. "They're still wet. I put them by the kiln to dry out."

Usher and Carlee engaged in small talk concerning the state of art in the economic scene as the cook went about her preparations. The calm was shattered by an unidentifiable crash, the slam of a door and the thud of a backpack hitting the floor and sliding into a door. Lindee was coming.

"Morning," she yelled. Oh, Rube, you're still here. I thought you are anxious to hit those Florida beaches."

Lindee had a fresh layer of paint on her face.

"Let's see that face," said Carlee. After a brief examination, she declared, "I think she'll be ready tomorrow."

"Good. I'll make the masks when she gets out of school tomorrow," said Usher. "Then I can hit the road early Saturday."

Carlee began ladling breakfast into large flanged soup bowls. She served the bowls along with a fruit cup of assorted berries.

Rube sat staring at his breakfast.

"Don't you eat grits either?" demanded Lindee.

"What are grits?"

"It's smashed corn and these are really yummy. Mom puts cheese in them."

Rube took a nibble and apparently decided they were edible and began his dedicated attack.

"I like my berries on top," said Lindee as she upended the cup on our grits. She made swirls with the various colored juices.

"Hey Rube," said Usher. "Yesterday when you had your things on the toilet tank I saw a good-looking drawing on a 3 x 5 card. Is that yours?"

Rube rolled his eyes up to look at Usher and said, "Uh, huh.

"What does it depict? I didn't recognize the layout."

A flare of pride came through as he said, "It's my own design for a tattoo that will start here." He indicated the base of his neck on the left side. "It will run around the shoulder blade and under the arm to the chest. The dot is where it goes around the nipple. It flows all around the arm down to the elbow."

Carlee leaned over the corner of the table to get her face close to Rube's. "If I ever hear of you getting that tattoo, I'll hunt you down and use my filet knife to cut all along the edge of that tattoo." As she clearly enunciated each word, she mimed holding her knife and slicing around the edge. "Then I'll pull that tattoo right off of you. If you are going to mutilate yourself, let's do a first class job."

Rube forgot to sneer. His eyes went wide. His eyebrows arched and his mouth fell open at the in-your-face-ferocity.

Lindee giggled. "You've had it now, the Carlee Curse."

No reply was forthcoming. Rube just dropped his head and started shoveling grits into his mouth.

"Hope you like grits," said Usher. "The further south you go the more you'll find them. In the south grits are called 'southern ice cream'."

Lindee rushed through breakfast and banged her way out to the bus stop. Rube went back to his reading.

Over their post breakfast coffee, both Usher and Carlee were keeping a surreptitious eye on Rube. Usher noted, "It would really be uncomfortable hitchhiking with wet feet in this weather."

"Sure would. How old do you think he is?"

"Fourteen, maybe 15. I'm not really the one to ask about kids. If he'd talk, you could probably better judge his maturity."

"I don't think he's that old. Lindee is 10 and it doesn't seem as if there's four or five years between them.

"I have to make a run downtown. Will you be all right

being alone with him

"I'll be fine. I don't sense any danger from him. Besides, he knows that you know he's here. Go whenever you want. I'll have Rube help me with the dishes."

CHAPTER 3

Usher drove off toward Albuquerque. Although, he was certain Carlee figured he was heading for a bank, he was really hunting for a Kroger's supermarket. That was the house brand that seemed most prominent in the cupboards. He also poked his nose into the freezer in the garage and found it was getting rather bare.

An inquiry got him going in the right direction. Upon arrival, Usher started at one end of the store and by the time he reached the other end, the cart was overflowing. Of course, by that time he had thought of any number of other items he should've picked up. Those will have to wait for a second trip.

He went through the checkout stand under the watchful eye of the manager. When Usher paid in genuine US dollars, the manager was all smiles and called a stock boy to help load the groceries.

Usher returned for another trip, which primarily focused on the frozen food situation. With a smile, he tossed four bags of peas into the cart. Also he picked up a couple of half gallons of chocolate almond ice cream.

When he returned to the house, he found Carlee in the studio. Rube was in filthy clay-stained jeans and a chambray shirt. He'd been cleaning the clay safe. .

"Hey, Rube, I need your help."

Rube trailed along with a disinterested expression on his face. His level of interest picked up somewhat when he saw the car load of food.

"Stack the stuff on the kitchen table or counters." Usher had opted for paper sacks so two-by-two the transfer started.

Carlee came out to see what was going on. When she saw what was being ferried in, the mandatory "you shouldn't have," became well overused.

"You've been feeding two extra hungry mouths with more meals to come," said Usher. "This represents only a fraction of what I would have spent if I had checked into a motel."

Carlee began separating the groceries. The frozen items went into bags that Rube carried out to the freezer. The sight of all those peas brought a frown that moderated when the chocolate-almond ice cream surfaced.

Usher wondered what the significance that chocolate-almond ice cream held for Rube.

Eggs from one of the cartons immediately went into a pot of water. Bags, boxes and cans disappeared into cupboards. Then she turned her attention to stocking the freezer.

Rube was sent back to finish wiping down the clay safe.

Carlee turned her attention to making egg salad, which ended in sandwiches... one for her and one and a half for the guys. Usher call Rube as Carlee served the coffee and milk.

The sneer had been replaced by a completely blank look that revealed absolutely no feelings.

In the two-way lunch conversation, Carlee asked, "What is your studio like?"

"I have the greatest studio in the world. It was a tough haul at first, but I was able to buy a commercial brick building in an older part of Denver. Gradually, that part of the city is being torn down to make way for modern office buildings. There are only two buildings on my block. The rest is all parking lots.

My building has a full, tall basement and two stories above. The basement is my studio. The first floor has two storefronts. I divided off part of the first floor and made an apartment. My tenant, Anasette, is a former ballet dancer, who was dropped on a leap, mangling her metatarsal bone, forcing a career change. Now she is a very talented jeweler. She has one storefront for dealing with customers. Behind it is her studio, sitting room, kitchen and bedroom. The other half is my storage and parking. That was until recently, Anasette came into ownership of a very valuable library on ballet and jade. I had to build a temperature and humidity controlled room to accommodate it.

"There is a loading dock off of the alley and a freight elevator that services all three levels. My place is on the second floor. The building runs east and west. When you get off of the elevator, my office and bedroom is to the right. If you turn left, there is a dining room and kitchen. Beyond that is the great room. This is an 80 foot free span gallery to display my work."

"Wow," explained Carlee. "I thought I was doing pretty good in the studio game. Someday, I'd like to see that studio."

"Hold on, there's nothing shabby about your studio. I can think of a whole bunch of artists of various kinds that would die to have your facility."

Usher had been keeping track of Rube's reactions. He still wasn't revealing any of his thoughts, but he hadn't missed a single syllable of the conversation.

"Oh, that reminds me," said Usher, "I need to call Anasette. She is expecting me back tomorrow."

"What kind of work does Anasette do?"

"You'll never run into a more creative person in a diminutive scale."

"Her or her work?"

"Both. She is petite with a great mane of black hair out to here." Usher touched the points of both shoulders. "She can reduce the whole world down to the size of a marble. She works the whole process from the idea on through to the finished piece, cast in either gold or silver."

****

Lindee had a talent. She could make a front door latch sound as if a jail door had just been slammed. As soon as she banged her way into the house, Carlee sent her off to get into her grubby.

Following the afterschool snack, everyone adjourned to the studio. "This is a home built kiln," said Carlee. "I designed it back when I was still throwing on the wheel. I can change the height depending on how much I have ready to fire. Now that I've changed my directions, I need to expand the width and length a few inches."

Usher had noted the kiln, but he hadn't given it any particular scrutiny. It was a rectangle with exterior dimensions of about 4 feet wide and 7 feet long. The exterior sides were concrete block. There would have to be an interior refractory lining. An insulated chimney went through the roof.

The top was made just like his burnout kiln. Two threaded steel rods ran through refractory bricks to form strips of bricks to bridge the width of the firebox.

The two females pulled on leather gloves. "Those bolts aren't really hot unless you have to hold them for a long while," said Carlee. "The threads can get to you, too."

Carlee positioned herself on the left side toward the corner of the studio. Lindee took the right side. The two hefted the first string of bricks up. Lindee walked around the kiln and they laid the assembly along the end wall.

Usher mentally winced. Those strings were not particularly heavy but for a small 10-year-old it would be close to her weight limit. Carlee had winced when she took on the load.

"Rube, grab Lindee's gloves. We're better equipped to handle that weight. Lindee get me a couple of hand towels. Your mom's gloves are too small for my big mitts."

The two guys quickly removed the top revealing the first wall plaque.

Carlee breathed a sigh of relief. "At least there is one good one. I don't know what I would do if they all cracked or warped. Usher, would you take the other end?" They lifted the first plaque out and laid it on carpet strips. Then Carlee removed all the kiln furniture revealing the second piece, which was also perfect.

The third had a blowout. "Oh, an air bubble."

When number four was revealed, Usher said, "Wow I was going to try talking you out of the one on the living room wall, but I'd rather take this one if it hasn't spoken for."

"No, it's not spoken for. You can have it."

"I have just the place for it, but I'll need another one with the bottom sloping off to the left instead of the right. I have two doors from my office/bedroom area. This will go over the right door."

When the four plaques were laid out on the floor, Carlee went over them minutely. They were about 14 inches high by about 40 inches long. She turned the damaged one on its face to inspect the back.

"There are more areas where I can reduce volume to lessen pressures. That should help the warping problem. The air bubble is just my sloppy work. I can live with a 75% survival rate."

Rube tried to feign indifference to the whole operation, but he never missed a thing.

Once the tension was released by unloading the kiln, Usher began to see the pressure Carlee had been under. She was thrashing around for a new area of creativity once the wheel was no longer possible. All adjourned to the kitchen area. Carlee put the coffee pot on for herself and Usher. She mixed a tube of frozen grape juice for the kids. Then she inspected Lindee's face.

"She'll be ready to go tomorrow if we can keep her from creating any other disasters."

"Good. I have to call Anasette. She was expecting me back this evening or tomorrow. I'll tell you what. I'll go out to the car to call Anasette. When I'm through, I'll toot the horn. If I can borrow Lindee to act as navigator, I'll spring for pizzas tonight."

"EEEE," squealed Lindee.

Rube controlled his expression, but he did straighten up from his tactical slouch.

"You don't have to do that," said Carlee

"I just want to celebrate the acquisition of a magnificent addition to my lair. Who likes what on their pizza besides peas for Rube.

Lindee laughed.

Rube almost cracked a smile before he could twitch his lip.

****

Before Lindee made it home from school, Usher retrieved his kit from the Shelby. He moved a long table away from the wall in the studio. He laid out his materials on the sink drain board.

When Lindee banged in the front door, Usher turned on the pot to melt the paraffin. By the time the afterschool snack was consumed and clothes changed, everything was ready.

The first item of business was to take a full set of head shots showing the face from all angles. With Lindee lying on her back, Usher applied a thin skim of Vaseline on her face and neck. He worked more Vaseline into the eyebrows.

"Now, I'm going to fashion two little plugs of plasteline with straws sticking through them. You'll breathe through them for a few minutes while I make the mask," said Usher. "I'll also make a couple of little wafers of plasteline to go over the eyes, just like they do with cucumber slices in those fancy spas."

Once the plasteline was in place, Usher continued. "Now I'm going to brush on a few layers of paraffin. It will be warm, but not enough to burn you. Hold still. Here we go."

Lindee flinched with the first swipe of the brush, but quickly settled down.

Once the first coat was on, Usher started adding gauze strips and more paraffin until he was satisfied with the thickness.

During the whole procedure, Usher kept up a running commentary on his activities and fielding questions from Carlee. Rube didn't make any comments, but he was an attentive spectator.

To cool down enough for removal, Usher draped a wet washcloth over paraffin while he removed the top of a shoebox. He scooped out some of the vermiculite into the lid of the box.

"Here we go. This is like opening the kiln. It's truth time." Ushered gently rocked the mold and lifted it off. The eye patches and nose tubes came away with the mold. "Do you have any eyebrows left?"

Lindee grabbed for her eyebrows. Usher handed her a tissue.

After an inspection of the mold, Usher proclaimed it to be perfect. He gently put it into the vermiculite. He poured a quantity of plaster of Paris into a rubber bowl holding water. When an island formed, he let it sit while he started cleaning up his mess.

Using a tongue depressor, Usher mixed the plaster into a smooth liquid that he poured into the mold.

"If it's all right with you, I'll stay tonight and pull out early in the morning," said Usher to the attentive mother.

"No problem. Your visit will be the highlight of our social calendar this year.

Usher laughed and continued. "It will be two or three weeks before I can send the finished mask to Lindee's dad. When I get home, I'll use wax to open the eyes, fixed the nose and do anything else I feel is necessary. From that I'll make another mold into which I pour wax to make a positive to take to the silversmith for casting. The time elements depend on how busy the silversmith is when I finish my work."

When the plaster in the mold had hardened, Usher poured the vermiculite back into the box. He taped the lid onto the box before storing it back into his case. He squeezed the rubber bowl to crack the unused plaster. The plaster shards went into the waste basket.

While Usher was returning his case to the Shelby trunk, Carlee brewed a fresh pot of coffee. The kids remained in the studio.

Usher took the opportunity to slide an envelope to Carlee. "Here's $1000 your ex directed me to give to you. Maybe you should ditch it while the kids are occupied."

"Good thinking." Carlee disappeared into the inner sanctum.

While she was gone. Usher wrote a check for the ceramic plaque.

"Don't forget my matching piece."

"Don't worry. I don't forget that kind of thing. Could I get you to go to the store for an unsliced loaf of Italian bread? Even though it was Pizza last night, it's going to be spaghetti tonight. Have to use the meat I thawed for last night.

"I suspected that, because of the aroma coming from that pot that's been bubbling away all day."

At the market bakery, Usher also picked up an angel food

cake. He added a couple of bags of assorted berries to his cart.

That evening, after the kids were asleep, Usher began collecting his things in preparation for an early start. Carlee was sitting at the dining room table so they could talk.

"I think your pound puppy is getting ready to disappear."

"I figured he would as soon as you pulled out, but why do you think so?"

"He's collected all of his things and returned that stack of magazines to their shelf. And this evening he gave your fairy houses another close inspection." What Usher didn't mention was that he slipped 4-20s into the pocket of Rube's jacket that was hanging on the hook on the bathroom door.

Carlee made no mention of the loaf of bread, jar of peanut butter and pack of individual raisin boxes she'd be leaving in front of the studio door.

When Usher's alarm went off, he nodded good morning to all of the eyes watching him and headed for the bathroom. Rube was already gone. When he returned to the house, Carlee was switching on the coffee pot.

"You didn't need to get up. I could've let myself out."

"Nonsense. You don't think I'm going to let you start off on that long trip without breakfast and your thermos full of coffee."

"Thank you," said Usher as he opened the valve on the air mattress.

"Leave that. Lindee will have time to take care of it. Did Rube leave?"

"Yeah. He's gone. I'm surprised he hung around as long

as he did. He seemed anxious to get down to the sunny beaches and free girls."

"He had to stick around until he found out what you're going to do."

"Me? Why?"

"At first he was very wary of you, but when he found out that you weren't a threat, curiosity took over. He had to find out why you are here."

"I rather suspect it was the three meals a day."""

"Of course, the kid is never going to pass up a meal but he could've helped himself to the larder or the freezer in the garage and disappeared that first night. No, I rather suspect he has always regarded males as a threat. He's probably always been the runt of the litter and he has been treated as such. The only thing you came down on him for was his attitude and he knows that stinks."

"I doubt that he has ever been around any creativity. That's what seems to fascinate him. I hope he finds a place for himself without being damaged too much."

CHAPTER 4

The sun was setting on the top of the Rockies as Usher pulled into his parking spot. When he stepped out of the Shelby, Anasette was leaning against the door jamb of her studio.

"Welcome back. I'll be up in 20 minutes and you can tell me all about your trip."

"Glad to be home. I have an interesting tale."

Usher made the mandatory checks of his studio, leaving his kit on the workbench. He took a freight elevator up to his living area. He paused long enough to visually survey the great room to make sure everything was in order, before heading to the shower. He fussed around in the bath until he heard Anasette's shower go off. He'd hear about it if he diverted the hot water so she got a blast of cold.

By the time the elevator returned to the first floor, Usher was in sweats and checking his answering machine.

The aroma of curry preceded Anasette, who was carrying a large oval Crockpot. She was dressed in her winter uniform...a floor length heavy, white, terrycloth robe and gray wool boot socks.

Anasette slid the Crockpot onto the dining counter and stretched up on the balls of her feet to offer her welcome home kiss.

"It proved to be a fun trip, but it's nice to be back home. Anything of interest happen around here?"

"Not much, except a small time jewelry manufacturer stopped by to see my designs. He got all excited over me instead of my work."

"I keep telling you about your powers over men," said Usher as he dropped the olives into their martini glasses.

"It wasn't for himself. He was looking for a wife for his son. He really liked the thought of having my talent in his family."

"My, that's a new approach. Did he show you a picture of his son?"

"Eh, it didn't get that far. He assumed I was Jewish and when he realized his error, he had lots of backtracking to do."

"And I bet you didn't make it easy."

Anasette gave him a benign smile as she sampled her martini. "You said you had a tale to tell me."

As Usher prepared the rice steamer, he began the Rubstory. It lasted clear through dinner.

"Carlee sounds as if she's quite a woman. While I clear away the dishes, go get her plaque. I'm anxious to see it."

Usher made the trip to the car for his new treasure. Anasette was as impressed with Carlee's creation as Usher had been.

Anasette ventured the belief, "I think she has a winner here if she can control her production."

"There was a call from Tanner. He asked me to give him a call when I came in. Let's see what he has in mind." Usher put the speaker phone on the counter after he punched in the number.

Tanner Jones was a valued friend of both Usher and Anasette. They considered him to be one of the great people of the world. His unfailing friendship, generosity and creative mind set him far apart from all others.

"Hi Tanner. You rouge. What have you been up to? Oh, Anasette is here too."

"Hi Anasette. What new great and wondrous things are you creating now?"

"Nothing wondrous, since I don't have any of your magnificent cabs."

Usher smiled as his petite friend making an oblique plea for more of Tanner's cabochons.

Tanner ignored the fishing trip. For the last week I've been in Portland helping Lyyli put the finishing touches on her book. The disc went to the printer this morning. It's going to be great. There's never been a book like it about the Lower Columbia.

"Actually, the reason I called was to alert you to the arrival of a little package. A while back, I was trimming up a piece of bloodstone. Misha talked me out of a chunk. He's graduated from button sized carnelian knots to golf ball sized bloodstone knots. The first one is for you. Boy, he's getting good."

"You mean you're giving away my trimmings," pouted Anasette.

"I'll be getting some more bloodstone," said Tanner. "I have a friend who owns a rock shop in Eugene. A couple of tons of bloodstone is being shipped in from Brazil. The best bloodstone comes from there. When the shipment arrives, Misha and I are going to pick out the best pieces. It'll probably take us a couple of days to shift through 4000 pounds of rock."

"I'm anxious to see that new piece," said Usher. "He's getting to the point you should find an outlet for him."

"This piece never was for sale. From the instant he saw the shape, it was always for Usher. He knew what was hidden in that little lump."

"He has a tendency to place little value on his work. That way he can give it away without any qualms."

Not wanting to press that subject too hard with Tanner, who had the same tendencies, Usher change the subject. The other day your name was bantered about in a strange way."

"Oh really."

"I was in Albuquerque on a job when a kid, who was obviously a runaway, drop by to raid the garden for a couple of tomato nubbins and a carrot. The homeowner said she had a soft spot for pound puppies and took him in for three nights.

"When I mentioned your name in a story I was telling, I got a definite reaction, although he denied knowing you."

"That may not mean much. My name is known fairly widely around here. What's he look like?"

"I'm guessing he's a small 14 or 15. Unless he grows out of it, he'll be incredibly handsome. His big claim to fame is his expertise with a Rubik's cube. He called himself 'Rube'.

"He doesn't seem to be anyone I know. It's time I started to think about dinner."

"What's for dinner?" said Anasette.

"Yesterday, there was a minus tide. Since Misha and I were on the coast, we dug razor clams.

"Oh," said Usher was feeling. "Ever since you fed me razors, I've been lusting after them."

"Why am I feeling left out of this?" said Anasette.

"Don't try razors if you plan on continuing to live in Denver," said Usher.

After hanging up the speakerphone, Usher freshened their drinks and the pair retired to the Great Room.

A few minutes later the phone rang. Usher let the answering machine pick up the call until he heard Tanner yelling, "Hey, Usher pickup."

"What's up Tanner?"

"When I hung up, I turned on the TV. The lead news story is about the manhunt for Topi Mannisenimäki, nicknamed 'Rube', who brutally murdered his foster parents by bashing them into a pulp with an aluminum bat. I called my friend, who is the night bartender at the Elks. He says your old friends, Sheriff Ballard and District Attorney Stanley are going to ride this kid to their reelection in a few weeks."

"Are you're sure it's the same kid? This doesn't sound right."

"The kid is actually 12 years old, who looks older. Good-looking and a whiz with a Rubik's cube."

"What happened?"

"The kid lived on a farm with seven other foster kids. On Monday they all went to school on the bus. Rube apparently skipped out of school, stole a car, went back to the house and bashed in the head of the foster parents, stole money and then dropped the car in Portland."

Usher sat in stunned silence. "Usher? Usher, you still there?"

"Yeah, yeah. I'm still here. This isn't right. The kid that spent three nights in Albuquerque didn't bash in anyone's head two days earlier. He is a snarly, snappy little twerp, but no murderer." There was another silence. Then Usher said, "Can you get word to your state police friend that Rube left Albuquerque before dawn this morning. He's headed for Cocoa Beach, Florida. This has to be straightened out, but I don't want to give him to Sheriff Ballard."

"Ballard will still get him. This is the sheriff's case. I'll have Lieutenant Kaddis track him down. I'll keep you posted."

Tanner's call really ruined Usher's night. He recounted the news to Anasette, who agreed that the situation should be dealt with as soon as possible.

"You've been saying that he is an arrogant, ill humored little bastard. Now you're saying he didn't murder those folks. How do you know?"

"My main source of disbelief is just being around him that long. I think I would have noticed something. A 12-year-old can't cover that kind of guilt for that length of time."

Anasette knew well Usher's sensitivity to others, but to help him crystallize his fragmented thoughts, she pressed on.

"Intuitive feelings would never stand up in court."

"Oh, there are other little things. He was grungy and smelly when he arrived in Albuquerque. Carlee washed his clothes. If he'd bashed in a couple of skulls, he didn't do it in those clothes. One of us would have noticed blood.

"I didn't count his money, but I bet there was no more than five bucks and a little change. I bet he hadn't been eating in restaurants or even fast food places.

"He was hiding a lot, but not extreme criminal activity. He was intensely curious about any creative activities. As Tanner would say, 'That kid has a head on his shoulders'."

Anasette laughed. That was the highest compliment in Tanner's repertoire. "Tanner'll keep track of what happens."

Three days later, Tanner called to report Rube was already back in Tillamook. He then was picked up in El Paso on Sunday.

"Minutes after the call came in that Rube had been picked up," said Tanner, "Sheriff Ballard was out the door headed for Texas. Rube was brought back as a runaway where he has no legal status. He wasn't charged until he was in Tillamook County."

"What's happening now," said Usher.

"Since he is so young they can't keep him in our jail. He is in the juvenile detention home. The Sheriff and the DA are both blabbing too much. They're making political hay."

"Nuts."

"The big argument now is if they can try a 12-year-old as an adult.

"Does he have representation?"

"A kid who has just passed his bar exam has been appointed his attorney. I don't know the guy."

After Tanner's call, Usher was in a foul mood. He passed

it on to Anasette. Neither had any interest in cooking, so Anasette's suggestion that they drive down to Dos Amigos for dinner seemed like a brilliant idea. "Maybe Maruca can cheer us up," said Anasette.

Maruca spotted them while they were still framed in the doorway. "Amigos, where have you been? Have you abandoned poor Maruca? I have not seen you in ages." As she glided across the room, she was throwing hand signals in all directions, animating the staff. The big round private table by the kitchen was being transformed from a restaurant set up to a more homelike atmosphere with a tablecloth, better flatware and service items. Another person was making fresh coffee.

Maruca was a youngish 30-35-year-old Mexican woman. Their paths had crossed when the artists were having a private art show in the famous old whorehouse. Maruca was a former prostitute, who was invaluable in unraveling an old murder. She had become an ardent follower of Usher's exploits. Her bright, shiny personality made her a joy to be around.

As usual, Maruca dictated the menu depending on who was cooking, which items were the freshest and best. That night it was calamari.

During dinner, their hostess dragged Rube's whole story out of Usher. The normally cheerful expression had gradually turned down. "Oh, pobre perito...poor puppy. He's too young to be all alone."

"Maruca," cried Anasette. "We came here to be cheered up and now I feel worse."

Usher didn't say anything. His expression needed no explanation.

"But the other side of the peso is the joy you will bring to your little friend when you find out who really killed those people.

Usher shook his head. "That's a novel thought. I'd been contemplating providing him with a decent attorney. I don't know what I can do from half a continent away and with no status in anything."

"You'll think of something," said Maruca, as she bounced up to head for the kitchen. Moments later, she returned with a tray holding three Mexican olles, mugs, which contained Presidente Brandy. "We will drink to Usher finding the killers."

CHAPTER 5

Periodically, Usher called Tanner to get the latest news. Unfortunately, there was little news except that the sheriff and district attorney were loudly campaigning to have Rube tried as an adult due to the excessive brutality of the murders.

Tanner was doubtful any local attorneys could help Rube. They were too tight a cabal.

Usher wasn't getting very much work done. He forced himself to finish Lindee's mask for her father. It was now at the silversmiths.

Sunday night, Anasette had come up to the great room for a glass of wine before retiring when the phone rang. It was too late for a boiler room call or for client calls, so Usher checked the caller ID. It was Tanner.

"Hi Tanner. You find any good bloodstone?"

"Sure did. Misha and I got back about an hour ago. As

soon as I entered the house I knew someone had been in here. I went over the whole place. The intruder snooped into everything. Apparently, he stayed here Saturday night and left out one door as we were coming in the other. The TV is still warm."

"Are you in any danger?" said Anasette who had been listening over the speakerphone.

"Don't think so. I know who it was."

"Who?" said Anasette.

"Your pound puppy."

"Rube?" said Usher.

"Misha was checking his room and noticed that his favorite shirt was missing. Several other items were gone. And in the back of the closet was a ball of clothes like the kids wear at JDH. I called my sister. Rube disappeared out of JDH Friday evening. They still don't know how he got out.

"I called my bartender friend. Our beloved sheriff and DA are beside themselves. I'm surprised you can't hear their screams of anguish from there."

"I'll go up on the roof to listen," said Usher as he chuckled. "He's on the run now, not just a runaway."

"I think he's headed your way."

"My way. What makes you think that?"

"He was into my computer. Your card was the last entry called up from my address book."

"Oh boy. Have any other suspects surfaced?"

"No one is looking. They think they have the right guy. I haven't reported the break-in. I don't want the sheriff snooping around my place."

"Well, thanks for the heads up."

"Incidentally, I was talking with Lyyli. She recognizes Mannisenimäki as one of the old River Finn names...for whatever that's worth."

"I wondered about that when I heard his name. Thanks."

Wednesday morning, Anasette went into her storefront to do some paperwork. As she settled down at her desk, she was aware of voices on the street. Since they didn't pass on, she peeked out of the blinds. A Denver patrol car was sitting at the curb with his blue lights flashing. A uniform policeman was standing over a figure of the kid sprawled over the hood of the car.

The figure turned out to be a small boy who looked as if he was dripping wet.

Rube. That was Usher's Rube. Anasette pulled the fluffy white robe around herself and stepped out the front door.

"Rube? Rube is that you?"

The figure gave the bob of the head.

"What's up officer?"

"I found this kid snooping around the building."

"He's a friend of my landlords, who is out running errands, but I'll call him to see what he wants to do. I'll be right back."

Anasette returned to the office to call Usher cell phone. When he answered, she said, "Your pound puppy is draped over the hood of a patrol car in front of the building. Do you want him?"

"If the officer doesn't know who he has, see if you can rescue him. I'm about 20 minutes away."

Anasette reluctantly went back out into the cold. "Officer, my landlord is about 20 minutes away and he'll take care of the kid."

"Are you sure you want this smelly thing?"

"Is that him that I'm smelling? It smells like rancid cooking oil, rotten meat and spoiled vegetable matter. I don't imagine that you want that stinky thing in your car. I know I don't want him tracking through my place. If you could march him around to the loading dock I'll take him into my landlord's area he can deal with his own problem."

Without even waiting for the patrolman to make any decision, Anasette wheeled around and entered the building.

Anasette's back door opened into the indoor parking area. Just past the elevator was a heavy door to the loading dock. Before going to the door she veered over to the box storage area and grabbed a large cut off box. When she got to the door she could hear activity outside.

As Anasette opened the door, Rube was coming up the steps to the dock. The officer stayed on the ground at a distance.

"Rube you're still dripping." Anasette dropped the box just inside the door. "Stand in this box."

The little jeweler smiled ruefully at the officer and gave him a wave. "Thanks officer."

She closed the door and stepped away from Rube "How did you get in this condition?"

"It was too late and cold to find this address, so I climbed into a dumpster that was by a warm exhaust vent of a Chinese restaurant. I was asleep when somebody threw a big, plastic garbage sack into the dumpster. It broke when it hit me."

"It's too cold to stand around out here. You're Usher's problem, so you can use his shower. Strip all those clothes into the box."

Rube was beginning to shiver violently. He shrugged off his backpack and began to remove his oil saturated clothes. He stopped when he got down to the skivvies..

"Those too. You're in an art studio. There are always nude models around here. I've seen it all.

"Oops, maybe I haven't seen at all. Oh well, it's too late now. It doesn't make much difference how many times one sees the same thing. Grab that box and follow me."

Anasette held the elevator door and her breath as a little blue kid carried his box into the elevator.

They turned right through the door into Usher's bedroom and office suite. The special thermalpane windows ran all the way across the end wall giving a panoramic view of the Denver skyline and the Rocky Mountains. In a bathroom on the left, Anasette stopped by the laundry.

Take all the stuff out of your pockets and backpack and dump everything into the washer." There wasn't much. There was a flatware knife, a jam jar, and part of a loaf of bread and the Rubix cube in the pack. There were a few coins in a pants pocket.

Anasette pointed that the shower. "Wash your hair twice and keep washing until you run out of hot water. There are towels on the shelf.

The shower went on. Anasette dumped soap into the washer and dialed "extra wash" before heading to the kitchen. The coffee maker was gurgling its last when the garage door open and closed. Shortly the elevator descended.

When the Usher rounded the corner of the elevator, the shaft of his nose was wrinkled. "What is that awful odor?"

With a smirk, Anasette announced, "That's your double murderer. At the moment, he's using your shower to freshen up."

"What happened?"

"You know the Chinese restaurant down the street that always smells like rancid grease? Rube was sleeping in their dumpster when a cook chucked a garbage sack. It broke."

"Oh boy."

"It was probably fortunate. The policeman didn't want to put that stinky thing into his patrol car."

Usher walked behind the counter to get the coffee mugs. As he was pouring the coffee, Anasette said, "There is something that you should know. Don't get in a tool measuring contest with him. You'd lose. That may partially explain how a 12 year old would look as if he is 14 or 15."

At that moment, the shower shut off. Shortly, a very hesitant little kid with a towel wrapped around his waist came around a corner. There was no sneer on his face. Rube advanced a couple of steps into the great room before he spotted Usher behind the counter. Turning toward the sculptor, the boy opened his mouth to say something, but nothing came out. He stood still for a moment before uttering a plaintive cry, the likes of which neither Usher nor Anasette had ever heard before. "Mr. Orlop, I didn't kill those two people, but no one will listen to me."

Then Rube's legs seemed to lose their bones. He slumped into a sitting position on the floor. The right knee stuck up in the air while the left leg was curled flat on the floor. Rube's right elbow was propped on his right knee. His hand grasped the top of his head as if he was trying to hold the contents in. The slack left arm lay across his left thigh and shin on the curved leg. The palm was up with his fingers slightly curved. It looked like the hand of a corpse.

Tears streamed down Rube's face, broadcasting the boy's utter terror.

Anasette started to slide from the stool to offer her comfort when Usher pinned her hand to the countertop. She whirled round to snap her objection when she caught sight Usher's expression. She knew that look. Creativity was brewing.

Under normal circumstances, Usher disappeared into a crowd. He was Mr. average. Being 6 foot, with nondescript brown hair and no particular distinguishing features, he passed through life pretty much unseen unless he was using his hands. When he was sculpting, drawing or fixing the kitchen faucet his hands became the featured attraction. For those who knew him well, there was another part of Usher, which commanded attention and speculation.

Anasette considered Usher's creative imagination to be one of the wonders of the world. When it kicked into gear interesting things could happen.

Usher slipped off his stool and passed behind the dining bar to his bedroom. Moments later he returned with his digital Elph.

The camera was set so there was no artificial click or warning light. Holding the camera about 18 inches off the ground, Usher and made a quick circuit around his subject, taking shots from all angles. Then he used the zoom lens to take facial features.

Rube was so deep into his private misery that Usher's action passed unseen.

When Usher was finished, he nodded for Anasette to proceed. Anasette also headed for the bedroom. When she reappeared she had another white terrycloth robe and a pair of long, gray socks. She settled down beside Rube and draped an arm over his quaking shoulder

Putting her head next to his, she said, "Rube, you want somebody to listen to your story. Now is the time to talk."

Gradually, the sobbing diminished and the eyes focused again. Embarrassment started to move into the forefront. He was sitting there bare-ass naked in front of a strange woman bawling like a baby.

"Come on, up you go." With her dancers grace she pressed herself into a standing position guiding Rube upright. She maneuvered Rube so his back was toward Usher. Anasette nodded as Usher took the standing, shot of the back from which he would figure the proportions for an armature.

Anasette held the robe for Rube. She pulled out a dining room chair out so he could put on the socks.

Usher poured a quarter of a mug of coffee and added another quarter of a cup of milk on top. Anything more than a half a cup would have been sloshed all over the counter.

As Usher headed for the office, Anasette guided Rube to a stool. "Take a couple of deep breaths and a drink of this. When Usher comes back, it will be time to tell your story. You couldn't have picked a better set of ears than his. He is very good at sorting through these things. If you want his help, don't leave anything out. The whole truth is necessary."

Rube bobbed his head in acknowledgment. He put his elbows on the counter to control the shakes enough to lift his cup.

Anasette heard the clatter of the printer starting up. Usher returned to the kitchen, taking his seat across from Rube, Anasette pulled her stool close enough so she had knee contact with the boy.

"Hi Rube. Tanner called to say we should expect you. You've come a long ways to have somebody to listen to your story. You'll have all the time you need to tell it. Let's start out at the beginning. Who are you?"

"My name is Topi Mannisenimäki. Both my parents are dead. That's about all there is."

"No, there's a whole bunch more. Is your name Finnish?"

"Yes."

"Do you speak Finnish?"

"No."

"Where are you born?"

"St. Helen's, Oregon."

"Is that on the river?"

"Yeah."

"Tell me about your father."

"His name was Otto. He was killed in a fishing accident just after I was born."

"What about your mother?"

"I don't remember much about her either. Welfare took me away from her when I was about five. I stole some county papers. They say my mom was a prostitute who would hook up with fishermen for a day or two or three while they were on the beach. She'd take me with her on those jobs. The guys would feed us. Somebody reported that and welfare took me away from her."

Pain tugged at Rube's face again.

"That must have hurt a lot," said Anasette.

"She was the only person I've ever had. In her way, she loved me."

"You say she's dead now, too?"

"Yeah. The report said she died of pneumonia in a little room in the back of a tavern. We stayed there when mom didn't have a job.

"Where was that?" said Usher.

"Astoria."

"How did you get to Garibaldi?"

"Years ago I was with a foster family who moved down there. My files were transferred to Tillamook County. I just stayed there."

"When did you go to the ranch?"

Rube looked up for a bit. "I guess it's about eight—nine months ago."

"Tell me about the ranch."

"All the kids know about the ranch. It's where all the worst kids go. If you're there, you must be bad.

"Why were you there?"

"I wasn't that kind of bad...either in trouble with the police or out of control. No one likes me, so I ended up there."

Usher made a mental note to follow-up on that later. "Go on about the ranch."

"It's way out in the sticks at the end of a long road. The bus driver hates to go out there but since there are eight kids, she has to.

"The place is run by the Hardys. The kids call Mrs. Hardy Mother Bear or MB...behind her back. MB was very unhappy when Mrs. Myers, the social worker, showed up with me."

"Why?"

"I was too small. She needed bigger, stronger kids to milk cows, make hay and work around the ranch. We were farmhands.

"The kids didn't like me either, because they felt they

would have more of a heavy work. They called me 'runt'."

"The rest of the kids were in school when I arrived. MB was furious after the social worker left. She finally cooled down. She mumbled that she would just have to make the best of it.

"All I had were school clothes so MB took me into a room where she stored clothes she picked up at garage sales and Goodwill. She told me to strip down while she searched for small work clothes."

Rube began to hesitate and fiddle with his mug.

"Go ahead, tell him," said Anasete.

"She made me take off my shorts. I am...I'm overdeveloped for my age. She said, "My, look what we have here." She started to play with it until he got hard. Then she wanted to know if it worked. She used my shorts to cleanup."

"You been teased a lot about that, haven't you?" said Usher.

"Uh, huh. I hate to go to gym class. It was even worse on the farm."

"How?" said Anasette.

"On the farm, there is a dormitory building for eight of us. There is a big room in the center to do schoolwork, watch TV, play cards. The computer is in there too. The boys" side is to the left. The first door is the boys' bathroom. The door at the far end goes back to four tiny bedrooms. Only Thumper's room has a door."

"Who is Thumper? said Anasette.

"He is the enforcer. He is called Thumper because he likes to thump on people. He makes everyone do what MB wants."

"Go on with your story," said Usher as he fixed a full cup

of coffee and milk for Rube.

"The kids came home from school just as MB was finishing up with the clothes. She was mad again because she was going to have to buy me smaller clothes. She didn't have much to fit me.

"She told Thumper to get me settled. Thumper doesn't do anything. Weasel is his strong arm back up and Raven is his girl. Those two suck up to Thumper and they do all his mundane jobs.

"Raven got a pillow, sheets and a couple blankets out of the closet for me. Wiesel told me I was to obey Thumper to the letter or I'd be sorry. He said I only had 10 minutes to get out of my school clothes and into the barn for chores.

"I was late because I couldn't keep my pants up. I finally found an extension cord.

"When I got to the barn, everyone was yelling at me because I was shirking my duties. Thumper threw a shovel at me and told me to go out to clean up around the manure trailer. All that stuff is shoveled through a hole at the end of the trough. The trailer was full and a lot of it ended up on the ground.

"When I got under the trough, Thumper and Weasel showed a great load of cow pee and crap over the back of my head. I had to go to where MB's caddie is washed and use the hose to clean myself before I could go to my room.

"Later Thumper caught me in the shower and yelled for Weasel. They started snapping me with wet towels. I tried to get away and went through a door into the living room where the girls were waiting "

"Did you continue to have a tough time with the kids?" said Usher.

"It was pretty much Thumper, Weasel and Raven against

the rest of us."

"How do you get along with MB and her husband?"

"Oh, Ed wasn't really MB's husband. To get foster kids you're supposed to be married. There have been several Eds."

"I didn't have much trouble with the Ed that was there when I was there. He did his job of running the ranch and Chirp and Willie kept him happy.

"What do you mean 'happy'?" said a suspicious Anasette.

"Whenever Ed wanted sex he'd have Thumper send him one. He couldn't keep them overnight on school days."

"What about the other two girls?"

"Oh, Raven was Tumper's private property. That's why Thumper had a door on his room.

Anasette bristled. "They had sex in there?

Rube shrugged, "Sure, several times a week. Then they go take a shower together."

"In the boy's side?"

"Sure...and showering isn't all they did in there."

Anasette decided not to pursue that line any further. She had enough information to raise her righteous indignation enough. The "private property" comment had almost been enough.

"What about the other girls?" asked Usher

"Gin was younger. He seemed to be saving her for a special occasion. He sent for her on Sunday, once in a while. It was just for a blow job-not to screw her."

The alarms sounded as the washer finish this cycle.

Usher nodded toward the laundry. "Rube, go dump your stuff into the dryer."

Without any reply, Rube slid off his stool and retraced the steps to the bathroom.

As soon as Rube was out of earshot, Usher shook his head while saying, "There's a whole lot here beyond a couple of murders. I wonder if the authorities know about this."

"Someone," said Anasette, "could view this as a strong motive for murder."

"Yeah. If any of this was officially known, I think some of it would have gotten out. Sheriff Ballard has too big a mouth to keep this quiet. The welfare..."

Rube was returning. Usher checked to see if the printer had stopped. He didn't want Rube to know about the photos at the moment. Usher still have some thinking to do.

"Rube. I suppose you could handle some lunch."

The subdued kid turned is very large baleful eyes on Usher and nodded his head.

"I have some roast beef and a good bread. Anasette, you have anything handy?"

I have some chicken stock. I could whip up a nice vegetable soup in a few minutes," said Anasette with a touch of hesitancy. Usher mentally grinned. She didn't want to miss anything.

"Rube. Take a break. Go look around the Great Room while we're getting things organized. We'll get back to your story after lunch.

Usher was curious about how Rube would spend his time. There was a chance he would fall back into his depression, but he rather doubted it. In New Mexico, curiosity had oozed out of him despite attempts to appear completely removed from the moment.

When Anasette returned with a steaming cauldron of soup, Usher had the sandwiches ready. He stepped around the kitchen wall to call Rube.

Rube was sitting cross legged on the floor in front of a 2 x 12 plank which was the display for the four18 inch sculptures of two young boys grappling with each other.

"Lunch," called Usher.

Rube responded immediately. "Those kids aren't trying to hurt each other are they?"

"No," chuckled Usher. "They're just brothers tussling."

"I didn't think so. Their expressions said 'play'. And in a couple of the fights it would have been over if you didn't mind breaking an arm or were going for the eyes.

"When you're a foster kid as small as me, you try to be prepared to take care of yourself."

Anasette was ladling the soup when they settle down at the bar. Usher noticed Rube checked the way things were done before joining in. Conversation remained on general topics during the meal. Rube maintained an open face and exhibited no unsociable attitudes, which was a far cry from what Usher had described to Anasette. His eyes kept darting around that part of the kitchen and those areas he could see from his seat.

Finally, Rube said, "Mr. Orlop, do you own this whole building?"

"Well, the bank and I do."

"Wow. Do you make your living doing that?" Rube nodded toward the great room.

"Those and masks like you saw me do on Lindee."

"Don't you go out to a job?"

"No, I work in my studio in the basement."

"You work at home like a farmer."

Both Anasette and Usher chuckled.

"Yeah," said Anasette, "I'm like a farmer too. I work at home too."

Rube blushed at having exposed his ignorance and mumbled, "I've never known anyone who worked at home other than farmers. I never thought about it before.

"Don't let it bother you. There are a whole bunch of things you'll never find in Garibaldi," said Usher.

Anasette began to clear the dishes. Usher poured coffee and said, "Okay, Rube, tell us about the day of the murders."

"There isn't much to tell. We all got up as usual on Monday morning. We did chores, ate breakfast, changed for school and caught the bus. We go to three different schools. When I got to mine, I waited outside until class started. I'd been watching a really short teacher's car. She had a booster seat to drive. She didn't lock her car either. It's had real dark windows. It was perfect. I hotwired the car and headed for Portland.

"I dumped the car in a factory parking lot and started hitchhiking south on I-5. I got to Albuquerque Wednesday where I met you.

"The popular theory," said Usher, "is that you stole the car, drove back to the ranch, killed the two and then drove to Portland. Did anyone see you that can testify that you were elsewhere?

"No. I avoided everyone. I was running away. I didn't even know about it until Sheriff Ballard told me what I did and how I did it

"That sounds like Ballard," said Usher. "Do you have any idea who could have done it? The other seven kids were in school. I can see why you're the suspect, but I would also expect there to be an investigation."

"The sheriff says he has all he needs to send me away for the rest of my life." Rube began to tremble. Tears welled up.

Anasette slid off her stool and put an arm around the boy's shoulders. "You're no longer alone. We'll straighten this out."

Rube tried to get control of his emotions again. Usher watched his face as he went through several of his playacting roles. None seem to work and ultimately he turned dark, baleful eyes up to Usher. "I didn't do it."

"Let's see if we can prove it," said Usher. "How does Ballard think you did it?"

"When I got to school, I stole the teacher's car and drove to the bus turnaround area by the house. You can't see that place from the farm buildings. I sneaked into the dormitory to get the bat. He says I went to the barn first and killed Ed and then went to the house and killed MB in her bedroom/office and stole the cash she kept in a drawer."

"How does he know you killed Ed first?"

"There were bloody footprints in the back door. It was Ed's blood."

"Then what?"

"I was supposed to have gone to my room and changed clothes. The bloody ones I was supposed to have ditched, buried or burned somewhere after I left."

"Were the footprints left by your size shoes?"

"The sheriff said the shoes were small. At the farm we

turned our shoes back in when they got too tight.

"The next pair might not really be the right size either. I don't think any of my sneakers are the same size. If they don't fall off, they fit."

"How much money were you supposed to have stolen and from where?"

"All the kids knew that MB kept money in the cash box in the top drawer of her desk. I don't know how much there was supposed to be. Neither does the sheriff. There was enough for our lunch tickets and grocery money. She gave Ed money for farm expenses and his personal stuff."

Usher cocked his head to listen. "Rube, the dryer just turned off. Go take care of your clothes."

When Rube vanished around the corner, Usher blew out a long breath. "Boy, there's a lot more to the whole affair than officialdom knows. That might be an advantage."

"I see your point," said Anasette. "I don't think he killed those people either. What are you going to do. Remember, he's still an escaped felony prisoner. And you are an adult male and he is a boy child."

"Yeah, I'm well aware that I'm walking through a mine field. But I have to do something. A couple of thoughts are floating around. As soon as we get the rest of the story, I need to do some thinking."

Rube came shuffling around the corner still dressed in a white robe and boot socks. He placed an arm load of neatly folded clothes on the end of the dining room table. His sneakers were deposited on the floor. "Is it's all right if I stay in the robe for the time being?"

"Sure," said Anasette, since the robe was her's.

"Tell us how you escaped and arrived on my doorstep."

Rube crawl back up on his stool and declined a refill on his coffee.

"They put me in JDH. There were a dozen or so kids in there...boys and girls. We weren't supposed to talk about our cases, but everyone knew that I was supposed to have killed two grown-ups. They were afraid of me. They thought I must have been a psycho case.

"After lunch all the kids were in the rumpus room. The counselor was leading everyone in playing games. I wouldn't play, so she sent me back to my room. I was locked in the boy's hallway. All the kid's doors were unlocked. I noticed the linen closet was unlocked so I looked in. That building had been something else before. All our rooms had solid ceilings but there was one of those ceilings made out of 2 x 4' panels. I crawl up the shelf and took a peek. The building has one of those European roofs." Rube described the shape in the air with his hands.

"A mansard roof," said Usher.

"There were four or 5 feet of space up there for plumbing, air conditioning and all that other utility stuff. Anyway, I locked the door, turned off the light and crawled into the attic. I returned the panel and walked down a pipe to the eaves. There were strips of plastic under the eaves. I set a couple of them aside and climbed down onto the electrical box. I replaced the plastic strips and hiked off into the woods.

"You went to Tanners? Why?"

"I knew he was a friend of yours and I needed somebody to listen to me. If he was like you, I figured he might let me tell my side, but he wasn't home.

"I rang the bell, but no one came. I follow the rope, but it didn't take me to the house...just out again."

"How did you get in?"

"I climbed one of the trees and I could see the roof. I broke a couple limbs, but I went overhead to the roof and dropped inside the fence."

"How'd you get into the house?"

"He's got a big workshop was all sorts of stuff. I made a couple of lock picks. That place is like a huge museum."

"Tanner said you made a pretty complete tour. How long were you there?"

Rube squirmed around on a stool and became pink around the edges.

"I didn't have anywhere to go. I decided to wait. That evening I ate some of his food. When it got late and he still didn't come home, I figured he might have gone somewhere for the weekend.

"I found the kid's room. I slept on his bed. The next morning Mr. Jones still wasn't back. I started to get scared he'd be mad at me breaking in and eating his food. I found your address and decided to come here. I took some of the kid's clothes and pack some of Mr. Jones' food in a backpack I found.

"I decided if he didn't come back Sunday night I'd stay over and leave early in the morning. But when I heard him coming in the back, I went out the front."

"Tanner called to say I should expect you," said Usher.

"How'd he figure that?"

"You left my address tab on his desktop when you put his computer back to sleep."

"Oh," said Rube.

Usher fussed with the coffee pot for a bit before turning his full attention back to the boy. "You know, Rube you have to go back to Tillamook to straighten this mess out"

Rube stiffened and then start to roll his upper lip.

"Smack." Anasette forcefully slapped her fingers along the edge of the bar making such a loud sound that both Usher and Rube jumped.

"Don't you dare curl that lip. You came here looking for help and you're getting it. It will have to be done the right way."

Usher said softly, "You know that as well as I do. Nothing can be done as long as you're a fugitive. Your side of the story is out now. There'll have to be a lot more proper investigation.

"You're too young to live on your own. No one will hire you so you can't get food and shelter. Have you ever been fingerprinted?"

"Yeah. Welfare wants them for identification."

"You can never do anything where you will be fingerprinted. If you ever get arrested for anything, you will be found out. With this hanging over you there is no chance for a normal life. Being a fugitive from a capital crime will be worlds worse than being a foster kid. You'll have to go back, but this time you will have help."

Despite Rube's terrified expression, he nodded his head with acquiescence.

"Hang on a moment. I'll show you part of my thinking." Usher headed for his office. A few moments later, he came back with a stack of letter size prints, which he lay face down on the counter.

"Rube, I took shameful advantage of you in a moment of great distress. My only excuse is that my mind works in strange manners. The instant you slumped to the floor, I saw a dynamic sculpture and moved to preserve the moment. I took this series of photos of you." Then Usher flipped the prints over and fanned them out.

Momentarily Rube blushed, but the content reactivated his despair.

"Rube. Rube," said Usher as the boy began to implode.

"Rube, does the name Jangala mean anything to you?"

"No."

"Jangala Lumber?"

"Yeah, I've seen that on boards."

"Yrlo Jangala, also known as the Little Tyrant, is a River Finn. Some consider him to be the patriarch of the Finns along the Columbia River. His family goes way back and his family was the most successful in the Columbia area.

"You saw the sculptures of the two wrestling boys in the great room?"

Rube nodded.

"They are River Finns too, I did those four little pieces and took the photos to Jangala, who helped solve their problem. Unless you object, I'll sculpt a piece from these photos and use it to bring your plight to his attention. I'll try to talk him into providing decent legal counsel. He has a flock of lawyers on call and I know there is at least one very expensive criminal attorney in the bunch. How does that sound?"

Rube stared at Usher for a moment before turning to Anasette, "Can he do that?"

"Yes," said Anasette with an encouraging smile.

Turning back to Usher he said, "You would do that for me?"

"Yes, but don't think it is all one way street. If Jangala takes an interest in your problem, I run a very good chance of selling him a bronze. That will go a long way to finance the rest of it."

"The rest of what?"

"What he means," said Anasette, "is there would be money to take care of airline tickets, car rental, living expenses... things like that."

"Oh," said Rube. These were considerations far beyond his experience level. He settled for just a bleak look.

"Would you object to me using these photographs to make a piece?"

"No," said Rube, "if you think it would help."

"There is no guarantee but I think it is worth the attempt."

"Okay."

Usher reached under the counter to turn on a CD player. He selected Venessa Mae and raised the volume a little above background sound.

"Rube, go visit the Great Room again while Anasette and I discuss some arrangements."

With a bob of his head, Rube slid off his stool and disappeared around the corner.

"What do you have in mind? said Anasette.

"I'm going to execute a plastaline figure about 24 inches high, photograph it and then take Rube back to Oregon. I'll try to sell Jangala on helping."

"If he doesn't?"

"Then I'll hire an attorney."

"That's what I thought. Then you plan on keeping Rube here until you do the sculpture. You know you're running a big risk. He's a felon fugitive, an adolescent male who you photographed in the nude without permission from anyone who can give such permission and then you're planning on taking him across state lines. I know your intent, but it may be hard to convince an enemy sheriff or self-serving district attorney of your pure intentions.

"Yeah, I know, but I can't put in a 911 call saying that I have a fugitive from a double homicide charge."

"I know that. What I'm saying is 'be careful'."

"I was hoping you'd take on the role of chaperone I also need a cook and a babysitter while I'm working.

"I suppose I can handle that for a limited time. What are you going to do with him at night?"

"He can use a cot and the bathroom in the studio. I don't have enough food in the place to keep the kid stoked. Are you all right with being alone in here with him or do you want to go shopping?"

Anasette fumbled with her empty cup for a moment. "Go do your shopping, I'll sit."

"Rube," called Usher. The white robed kid glided on silent feet around the corner causing Usher to wonder if Rube had some of the same inclinations as the wrestling boys... to eavesdrop on everything. Was that a Finnish trait?

"Rube, I'm going out to stock up on some food. Anasette is in charge. We are not going to advertise your presence here. That could lead to problems. It'll take me four days to a week to sculpt this piece. Then you and I will fly back to Portland to see Jangala. If you have a better plan, be ready to convince me when I get back.

"Anasette, would you check what I have up here, and what you have on hand and make out a shopping list? I want to weld up an armature so that it will be ready to use when

I get back."

Anasette's eyes flicked toward Rube.

"Come with me Rube. I'll show you where you'll sleep. This won't take long." Usher gathered up the photos and headed for the elevator with Rube in his wake.

Usher continued his scrutiny of Rube. It wasn't hard to watch because the boy was taking in everything within sight. He watched the opening of the elevator door, studied the control panel and examined the roof escape door. Rube was no conversationalist, but he was an astute observer. Usher wondered if that was a trait of foster kids who seldom felt they were secure enough to express themselves.

When Usher opened the elevator door to the total darkness of the basement studio, Rube held back in the lighted box until Usher switched on some lights. Rube had to step out before he could see the extent of the cavernous studio extending to the left.

"Wow!" said Rube, "this all yours?"

"Yep," said Usher with a touch of pride. "Don't get the idea that all sculptors have something like this. I've been lucky."

Usher led the way around the elevator to the other side where there was the rudiments of a bedroom where a few winks could be caught without going upstairs.

"There's a half bath through that door. You'll have to shower upstairs. You're going to have pretty much free run of my home and studio. Please honor that. Oh, another thing. Tanner was pretty much able to track your path through his place. Around here, there are any number of things that can leap out and take a bad bite. Be careful."

Usher turned on the lamp by the bed. "You can leave the bathroom light on as a night light. I need to get that armature done."

"May I watched?"

"Yes, but keep back while I'm welding. I don't know how fireproof those robes are."

Usher led the way through a large multipurpose room to a central corridor that went past numerous rooms with 4 foot solid walls and then topped with glass windows that ran almost to the ceiling.

Rube's eyes flitted along all of the windows. He wanted to ask questions but apparently wasn't sure enough of his status to engage in open conversation.

"When I was building my studio, a window glass manufacturer was doing a custom job for a new downtown commercial building. When the windows were installed they suddenly found out that the lower section that opened was supposed to open in instead of out. The sharp edges on the open windows were about 6 feet above the sidewalk.

"They remade the order and I bought the old ones for pennies on the dollar. It was cheaper to use glass than to build solid walls and I didn't have to install lights in each room."

Rube shadowed Usher down the central corridor past woodworking, painting and fiberglass to drafting. Quickly, the sculptor drew a stick figure on the back shot of Rube. Then, he measured his lines and multiplied them by an unknown factor resulting in figures being inscribed all over the print.

Usher's only comment was, "If you ever do anything like this, use the metric system. It's a lot easier."

They moved across the aisle to welding. "You better watch from behind the glass. Against the wall was a pile of iron rods. Using a tape measure stapled to the wall, Usher measured in number of pieces which were cut with a bolt cutter. The iron rods were laid on a bed of white brick in a stick figure but about four times larger than the photograph.

Usher fired up an oxygen/acetylene torch and quickly fused the pieces together.

Rube mentally cataloged each move the sculptor made. He'd never seen anything welded before but with a little practice he figured he could duplicate what he'd witnessed.

Using the other photographs, Usher began heating the metal cherry red and bending the rods into the shape of a seated Rube.

Usher stood back to review his work. He made a few changes before shutting off the torch and the gauges. This will be cool when I get back. Let's go see if Anasette has the list ready."

Since the elevator was coming from the first floor, Usher knocked on Anasette's door. Receiving a yell from the inside, the pair entered. "Have a list for me?"

Anasette smiled. "You bet. Since you're buying, I have a list."

Usher glanced down the long list. "How do you know if Rube likes shrimp and scallops?"

"If he doesn't, I'll give him a wiener and then there will be more for me.

Usher rolled his eyes. "Okay. Keep this young lad safe from Tigers. I'll be back as soon as I can." He left reading the elongated grocery list which included four of those hideously expensive chocolate desserts from the specialty bakery. Anasette was extracting payment for babysitting his problem.

When Usher returned, he yelled for Rube to help him transfer a car load of groceries to Anasette's.

"If you'll sort this out...send Rube up with what has to go into my refrigerator or freezer. I'm going to change clothes and start the piece."

"Can I watch?" asked Rube with the most vocal animation he'd yet exhibited.

"Fat chance," said Anasette. "He is a secretive old grouch when he is working on a piece. I don't even get to see them until he is finished."

Rube wilted a bit.

Usher watch the kid's reaction. "Since your bed and bathroom are down there, I'll make a deal with you. You come and go quietly...no conversation...you can do so. If you want to watch sit on that packing crate off to the side. No critical comments. Okay?"

"Okay."

"Young man, how did you get so lucky?"

Rube shrugged, but he carried a pleased expression, which was a massive improvement over his former snarl.

CHAPTER 6

Usher moved into his creative mode. The outside world only existed at the periphery of his consciousness. He was aware when Rube came and went. When he got hungry, he went to his pad. Normally he would have scratched together whatever happened to be available and the quickest. But most of the time there was a plate of whatever Anasette and Rube were eating sitting in the refrigerator. If he got too sleepy, he'd have to go to his own bed instead of crashing on the cot.

Somewhere along the line, Anasette called while he was eating. "Do you have any sheet copper?"

"There are some bits and pieces in the wall rack in the metal room. Help yourself."

"Thanks, I'll send Rube down for it."

"Thanks, for the food."

Usher heard the elevator leave in a bit. Someone sent it

back up to him.

Rube spent long hours sitting on his box silently watching. He also laid on his bed observing the process before dropping off to sleep. In the morning, he stayed propped against the wall until he heard Anasette moving about. Then, like a white ghost, he slipped away.

The end was in sight. Usher moved about the piece, touching up little spots here and there. He stood in front of it for a long look. He viewed it from many different angles. Suddenly, Usher reached out and grabbed the left up-turned hand and crushed and twisted plasteline off the armature.

Rube let out a very audible gasp. Usher shot him a sour glance. Rube tried to shrink into the folds of his robe.

Usher set about changing the angle of the forearm and reestablishing the hand. When the piece passed his final inspection, Usher took the elevator to his pad.

Below, Anasette was listening to the sounds of the building. "Usher's finished. About four o'clock he'll wake up, shower, shave, change clothes and then be ready for a martini. He'll be human again and you can talk to him."

"Is that how artists act?" said a baffled Rube.

"No, that's just Usher. Every artist has his special working habits. I'm probably even worse when I get on a creative binge."

At three o'clock Anasette put away her project. I'm going to get cleaned up. You can have a shower when I get out."

When Anasette vacated the bathroom, she tossed Rube a clean robe and socks. "Put the dirty ones in the washer. I'm going to take care of your shaggy hair."

Again Anasette was listening to the building...running water and squeaky boards. "Come on, let's go up."

When Anasette and Rube stepped out of the elevator, Usher met them coming out of the bedroom.

"I told Rube you'd be human again."

"Yeah, I think you're right. It's martini time. What day is it?"

"Sunday," supplied Rube.

I hope I can get everything arranged so we can fly out of here tomorrow.

Immediately, Rube started to fidget. He was becoming frightened again.

"Come on," said Usher, "this is what we've been working for. We have to go take care of this problem. It has to be done."

Rube nodded, but it still scared him.

Usher busied himself at the kitchen bar mixing a black Russian for Anasette and a Beefeater martini for himself. He also slid a tall glass of tomato juice with a dash of Tabasco and a feathered celery stalk across to Rube.

Both adults were watching how Rube handled the situation. He seemed pleased to be included in the group but the celery was causing him a problem.

Anasette leaned over. "Hold the green thing back with your forefinger so you don't lose an eye."

Rube handled the celery according to instructions but the Tabasco presented a new challenge. River Finns are not accustomed to picante. Outside of a lot of lip–licking, Rube made his way through his cocktail.

Through martini time, conversation had been along innocuous lines, but when Usher put his glass down in the sink, stating it was time to hit the phones, he signaled that the happy hour was over.

Rube immediately understood that adults had to do adult things. He excused himself to go down to his bed to try to finish some reading.

When the elevator descended, Anasette asked, "What did you do to that boy? When he came up here earlier, he was babbling about something and kept trying to twist his left hand."

"Oh boy. He saw me twist the hand off the figure so I could redo it."

"I told him something must not have been right. You go do your arranging. I'll scrape up something to eat. We're getting pretty close to the bottom of the barrel.

"You're going to have to buy Rube some new clothes. Misha's are much too large for him and the two of you wouldn't fit together in public unless you want to get some of Tanner's clothes to wear."

""Thanks. I don't want to take Rube outside right now. I'll take his measurements and hope for the best."

****

It had snowed during the night, so the roadways would be salted. Usher hated to take his classic Mustang out under those conditions, but the heater in the van was not up to keeping Anasette from getting cold and grouchy.

Rube was in the backseat in his new clothes. He'd been schooled to reflect a father/son relationship in public.

At the Portland airport, Usher rented a car and immediately headed for Lyyli's houseboat on a slough of the Columbia River, which was not all that far from the airport.

Tanner's left-leaning compact car was in the parking lot. Someone had been watching because Tanner and Lyyli stepped out onto the front deck as soon as Usher and Rube started down the ramp to the dock.

Rube's normal size inferiority complex around adults took a real hit when he was introduced to Tanner. Rubes tiny hand disappeared into an enormous mitt as he received the usual Tanner handshake.

Then Rube embarrassed himself when his eyes lingered too long on Lyyli's well-developed chest.

Everyone had a laugh at Rube's expense. Usher checked his watch. "I have to go. I don't want to be late for Jangala's appointment."

Usher timed his arrival so that he was punctual. Mrs. Kalunki answered his ring almost immediately, indicating she acknowledge his punctuality. There had always been an armed standoff between Usher and the aging house manager for Jangala.

"Mr. Jangala is in his office. This way please. Mrs. Kalunki performed her prescribed duties of presenting Usher before heading to the kitchen for the coffee service.

Yrlo Jangala hadn't changed since the last time Usher has seen him. He still looked like an old zoo lion that could no longer hunt. It was his eyes that belied the initial impression.

Never one to waste time or relinquish the dominant position, Jangala said, "Your message said that you had two items you wish to discuss."

"Yes sir. I presume you have a DVD player.

Jangala bobbed his head toward a large ornately carved cabinet to the right of his desk. "I watch DVDs on my computer."

Usher pulled a DVD case from his attaché case. He moved across the room to the cabinet. Behind the doors was a working desk and a new iMac with an oversized flat screen. Usher felt a twinge of jealousy.

The computer came out of his slumber as soon as Usher slipped a disc into the slot. Without preamble the screen filled with too little, blond boys in a galley kitchen surreptitiously poking at one another while their mother was occupied in putting things into a refrigerator. Eric, the 11-year-old, was reciting a poem while he was multitasking. He was washing dishes and defending himself from a rear attack of poking, jabbing and flipping from his 10-year-old brother, Jon.

"One evening," said Usher, "Anasette and I were invited to stay for dinner. Since we're old friends, the Pells joined us in the dining room. After dinner, the Colonels invited Anasette and me to go to their rooms for an after dinner drink. I left the video camera on the side board. This is all raw, unedited video. They didn't know these moments were taken.

"Eric is going over all he covered in school that day. It is discussed and then Jon does the same thing. The boys think their mom is a genius because of her knowledge about everything. What they don't know is that she spends a lot of time on the computer after they go to bed looking up better explanations or items to expand their knowledge.

"Incidentally, Brita could really use a good laptop that she can use in her room so that she doesn't have to sit in the living room half the night. They are within range of the colonels' router."

Jangala was intently watching and listening carefully to the interchange between English and Finnish. The boys used what Finnish they knew, but readily interjected English to fill in the blanks.

Little by little, Jangala was inching his castor chair closer to the screen.

"There's about half an hour of this." Usher went to the

computer. Jangala started to object to turning it off but Usher forged ahead and advanced to the second chapter. "These shots were taken through the colonels' security system. When they were under siege, they looked to their security with surveillance cameras. There is one behind the dressage ring.

"One of the first things the boys found upon their arrival on the farm was a large galvanized stock watering tank. It is about 3 feet high and 12 feet across. Immediately the boys engineered a way to get water back there. Colonel Polanski was particularly pleased in the inventiveness displayed. They even used the eve trough along the horse stable to move the water."

The camera showed a placid scene from the dressage ring past the water trough to the vast grassy pastures beyond. Suddenly shadows entered the scene. The afternoon shadows were attached to Eric and Jon who were shedding clothes as they ran. They delayed long enough to wiggle out of the remaining garments before hitting the water. Jon being the shorter, grabbed the rolled metal edge and swung himself up and over.

Eric gripped the edge and jackknifed into a handstand before laying over backwards into the water with a satisfying large splash. You're wrestling match immediately ensued.

"There is no audio with this camera," said Usher.

"Who is that?"

Oh, that's Ali. He is a little orphan who had no country and no love. Breta and the boys wiggled around a bit and made room for him. The colonels are footing the bill. Eric and Jon are water creatures like otters. Ali is a dry land creature like a horny toad."

"Another of your projects?"

"I suppose I could be blamed." Usher let the DVD run a bit longer. There's probably 30 to 45 minutes of photos through various cameras. This is yours to watch at your leisure."

Turning off the computer, Usher pulled four sheets of paper from his attaché case.

"This is where you want something," growled Jangala as he reluctantly returned to his desk.

"I suppose you could say that. This is item number two." Usher laid the front view of the Rube sculpture on the desk in front of the Little Tyrant. He lined the various other shots up above the first one. Usher returned to his chair and took a sip of his now cold coffee.

Jangala studied the photos for some time, occasionally moving his head slightly to deal with the glare of the glossy surface. He glanced at the various other prints and returned to the front one.

When Jangala finally looked up, he didn't say anything, knowing Usher was prepared to explain.

"Does the name Topi Mannisenimäki mean anything to you?"

"Topi Mannisenimäki," said Jangala, correcting Usher's pronunciation. "No."

"This is Topi Mannisenimäki, a 12-year-old, Columbia River Finn, who is wanted for the gruesome double murder of his foster parents in Garibaldi. I don't think he did it.

Jangala leaned forward to press a button on a console on the edge of his desk. To the "Yes, sir?" Jangala ordered a replenishment of coffee. He then leaned back to listen to Usher's story.

Even though Usher tried to keep it brief, the telling took a considerable time.

When Usher finally fell silent, Jangala said, "What do you want of me?"

"Rube...that's his nickname because of his expertise with the Rubik's cube...is being represented by a kid who has just passed his bar exam. He is working in a poor county, who has little to pay public defenders and he has to face a district attorney and a sheriff who plan on riding this case on to their re-election.

"I know you have a battery of attorneys available to you and at least one is a competent criminal lawyer. I can't remember his name, but he handled your grandson's affair for you. What I am asking is that you provide for Rube's defense."

Jangala reached for the phone. When his ring was answered, he said, "Mrs. Kalunki please get Frans Huuskonen on the phone."

As the old man waited, Usher said, "I can have his client here in about half an hour."

Jangala's attention returned to the phone. "Mr. Huuskonen, I am sending you a 12-year-old client named Mannisenimäki. Please arrange defense for a double homicide in Tillamook County. Mr. Usher Orlop will bring him to your office in about an hour."

After listening to the response, Jangala said, "Thank you," and hung up.

"The boy is here?"

"He will be shortly, excuse me." Usher dialed his cell phone. "Tell Tanner to bring him."

Usher flipped the instrument closed. Tanner Jones is bringing him over. You may recall the name. Asti dynamited his compound. Another item of interest...Tanner has the grand steel entry arch from the River Lights Hotel in front of his Driftwood Forest. It is quite a tourist attraction. I lined my great room and the front of my studio with some of the smaller arches.

Jangala took note of the information but something else was commanding his attention. He was silent for a bit before asking, "When will you bring Eric and Jon to see me?"

"That will be a decision for Brita to make. Right now, the name Jangala is closely related with the scariest event of their lives. In a few days, Lyyli's book on the lower Columbia will be out. When the time is right, Brita plans on giving the book to the boys. I understand your name comes up frequently...not always in the best light.

"I can imagine," growled Jangala. "However, I probably earned the comments. Who is Lyyli.?"

"Lyyli Linx. She is one of your River Finns but she traded her unpronounceable name to its translation. It looks better on her paintings."

"A painter? Is she any good?"

"Very good."

"What is this book deal?"

"For years she has been chugging up and down the lower Columbia in an old day-fisher painting riverscapes and collecting historical material. Your grandson actually started this whole chain of events. Tanner found Lyyli while investigating those iron arches. When the Pells' house was a destroyed, I got Lyyli to smuggle Brita and the boys upriver. She hid them for several weeks. During that time, Brita knocked the rust off of Lyyli's Finnish sufficiently so that she felt competent to interview the old people who spoke little or no English.

"When the boys get their hands on that book, they will have a much better understanding of where they come from. When those two little guys turn their eyes in your direction you may well feel their gaze even at this distance. They are getting quite good on the computer and Google is their playground.

"Mr. Orlop. I said I would not interfere with their lives but you can see that my time is getting short. I appreciate the video and the reports but I would very much like to take their measure in the flesh.

"Now that the new business world has passed me by, there is little to occupy the mind and the time."

"I'll relay your concern to Brita," said Usher as he went to the computer. He brought up the word processing program. He opened a new document entitling it "The Jangala Story", create a file folder and save it to the desktop.

Returning to his chair, Usher said, "When you get lonely, bored, hurting, worried or sleepless work on the Jangala story. You'll be surprised how time just vanishes. And consider that there is no one else in the world who can tell your story."

Jangala started to object, when the door chime sounded. A short time later Mrs. Kalunki opened the door to admit the new arrivals. Tanner's immense bulk dwarfed Rube. Tanner nudged Rube forward. Deprived of his playacting personas, Rube was a terrified little boy, especially after he spotted the grizzled old man staring at him from behind a massive ornate desk.

"Mr. Jangala, may I present Tanner Jones and Rube?" Usher wasn't going to bungle Rube's name a second time.

Tanner stepped around Rube and quickly closed on the desk. In typical Tanner fashion, he stuck out his right hand catching Jangala by surprise. The old man's hand raised from the desk in reflexive reaction. Before he could withdraw the unruly hand, it disappeared into Tanners enormous paw.

"Mr. Jangala, I'm truly pleased to meet you. Your name has commanded much of my attention recently." Tanner gave Jangala a good manly handshake without causing any distress to the ancient bones.

Usher had to restrain a grin. Jangala probably hadn't shaken hands in several decades. During that little byplay, Rube had come to stand next Usher. When Tanner retreated to a chair, Jangala turned his attention to the boy. Usher pulled a jumbled Rubik cube from his attaché case. He flipped it to Rube. It seemed as if the queue started to order itself while still in the air because Rube was handing it back moments later. Usher leaned forward and placed the rearranged cube on the corner of the desk.

"What's your name boy?"

"Topi Mannisenimäki"

Topi Mannisenimäki," corrected Jangala. Mr. Orlop tells me you're being falsely accused. Is that true?"

"Yes, sir."

Jangala continued to stare at the boy.

Rube fidgeted under the steady, unblinking gaze. He glanced at Usher and Tanner but neither offered any guidance or relief. Rube faced Jangala's emotionless face. He straightened his back and pulled his shoulders up. "I didn't do it." As an afterthought he added "Sir."

"Good," said Jangala. "Mr. Orlop will now take you to see my attorney and then you must go back, so this affair can be resolved. Your story has been heard. Now you must be patient."

The grizzled head bobbed toward Tanner. "Mr. Jones."

Jangala bent over the photos before him.

The trio had been dismissed.

Before they could exit, Jangala said, "Mr. Orlop, is number one available?"

"Yes."

"Send it to me."

"As soon as it can be cast."

Under the portico, Rube's backpack was transferred to Usher's rental car.

"I'll save some dinner for you," said Tanner as he turned his sad looking compact toward home.

Usher unfolded a Portland map and had Rube find the attorney's address as they wound their way down the mountain. When Usher found the law offices of HHG&H he knew why they use initials. Most Portlanders would have foundered on all those Finnish names. He paid particular attention to Jangala's pronunciation of the one they were supposed to see, so he wouldn't embarrass himself too much.

Frans Huuskonen was waiting for them. Obviously, there had been another conversation with Jangala. As soon as everyone was seated in the attorney's posh office, Usher launched himself into telling Rube's tale. This was done to save time and to prevent Rube from having to again relate all those embarrassing events.

Mr. Huuskonen periodically looked to Rube for confirmation of points. Rube would nod his agreement with the statement. When Usher finished, the attorney questioned Rube more closely concerning his activities on the morning of the murders.

Turning to Usher, the attorneys said, "Mr. Jangala said

you would probably have some suggestions on how to proceed."

"We are headed for Tillamook. As soon as I show up at JDH, I'll probably have a confrontation with Sheriff Bosco Ballard. He doesn't like me now and when he finds out I'm putting his reelection in jeopardy, he really won't like me. I need a letter appointing me as your investigator with the authority to collect copies of the incident reports and crime scene photos and any other items you are normally entitled to.

"I will then have a chance to take a look at them. Whoever killed those people had to know about the operation. Maybe I can come up with an alternative suspect. I'll forward the files onto you."

It took some time to get a letter typed and several copies notarized and information exchanged. Just before they left, Rube was again admonished by Huuskonen. "Remember, don't discuss any phase of this case or any of your travels, including your escape and return with anyone without me being present. The only exception to this is Mr. Orlop."

"Add Tanner Jones to that list. He is helping me and Rube knows him. Also, Tanner can be extremely helpful. He's a knowledgeable local."

"Okay," said the attorney. "Just those two. If anyone else wants to talk about it hand him or her one of these cards and have them call me." Huuskonen stuffed a stack of business cards into Rubes shirt pocket. Usher also picked up a supply.

By the time Usher pulled up to JDH, the front office was closed. They had to ring a night bell. It took a while for a house parent to get through all the locked doors to the front entryway.

Over an intercom a middle aged woman said, "The office

is closed until 8 AM."

Usher tugged Rube forward. "I think you lost this one. I'm just returning him."

The woman bent forward to get a better myopic look through the glass. "Oh, oh, he's the one that escaped. Don't leave. I have to get a key."

The woman fled into the inner sanctum.

"There's only two adults here at this hour. One always has to stay in the back if there are any kids here," said Rube. "I don't know this one."

The male house parent hurried into the reception area with a key in his hand. When he managed to get the door open, Rube said, "Hi, Mr. Miller, did you miss me?"

"You really caused a sensation around here."

"Mr. Miller, my name is Usher Orlop. I represent Topi Mannisenimäki's new attorney, Frans Huuskonen of HHG&H in Portland. Here is a copy of the authorization letter. Would you please write out a receipt showing the time, date and location of my surrender of Topi to your custody. Handwritten on office stationery will do."

Usher picked up a pen from a holder on the receptionist's desk and handed it to the house parent, who was beyond his depth. He moved to comply with the request. He had to ask how Rube spelled his name.

While waiting for the receipt, Usher said to Rube, "You're not going to need that shirt now. Take it off. I'll return to Misha. That's his favorite work shirt." Rube stripped off his outer shirt and handed it to Usher.

Usher removed the attorney's cards from the pocket before tucking the shirt under his arm. He exchanged one of the cards for the receipt from Mr. Miller. The rest he gave back to Rube.

"Mr. Miller, Rube is under strict orders from his attorney not to discuss any phase of this case with anyone without the attorney being present."

Usher listened for a moment. "It sounds as if your dear sheriff is about to put in an appearance. I'd rather confront him outside. Rube you hang in there. This may take a while, but things are moving in the right direction."

Rube was frightened, but he hung in there. "Thank you Mr. Orlop. His hands were trembling as he stuck one out for a handshake.

The boy really needed a hug, but Usher knew that wasn't the time or place for it.

Usher was leaning on the fender of a rental car when Sheriff Bosco Ballard came slithering into the parking lot. He was no longer using his siren, but the blue light was still winking.

Ballard swung around so his headlights were directed at Usher, cutting through the evening gloom.

"Orlop? Orlop, what the hell are you doing here?"

"Oh, I just returned your lost kid."

"How'd you get involved in this?"

"Sheriff, I don't know how you do it, but you always seem to be on the losing side. Rube didn't kill those people."

"What do you know about it?"

"I'm Rube's new attorney's authorized agent. I'll be stopping by your office about 10 o'clock tomorrow morning with a letter from the attorney to pick up all pertinent incident reports and crime scene photos. So to save time, you might want to get somebody working on it now."

"I'm not about to turn anything over to you."

"Check with your DA buddy. He'll tell you the law. Incidentally, Rube is under strict instructions not to talk to anyone without his attorney being present.

Usher handed the sheriff an attorney's card. "Of course, between us old friends, it would be a waste of time because Mr. Huuskonen would tell Rube not to say anything."

"The kid already has an attorney."

"Rube decided this one is better. He is one of Jangala's attorneys."

"The lumber company?"

"No, Yrlo Jangala's personal firm."

"The Little Tyrant? How'd he get involved in this?"

"You're screwing around with a River Finn. He takes a dim view of that."

"That's too bad," snarled Ballard. "I've got a case and I don't care how many high-priced attorneys that he runs in. I'll get my conviction."

If you don't get a conviction, that wouldn't bode well for your reelection would it? If you get busy and come up with the real killer you might still salvage something."

"I can take care of myself," said Ballard. "I'm going to check on you. If you are misrepresenting yourself, you'll have your own charges to worry about."

"It's past my dinner time. Have those reports ready for me at 10:00." Usher levered himself upright and unlocked the door of his car.

The Sheriff muttered something under his breath as he moved to the door of JDH.

CHAPTER 7

The gate to Tanner's compound was open. Usher drove around to the back of the house and returned to lock the gate before going inside.

Tanner nodded to a mug of coffee on the counter. "How'd it go?"

"Little Rube is scared to death."

"He has every right to be. The world's been stacked against him as far back as he can remember. Kids like that are survivors."

"Somebody called Ballard. I could hear his siren just minutes after we got there."

Tanner got a wolfish grin on his face. "Did he try to arrest you?"

"I didn't give him a chance. I told him I was representing Rube's attorney. We'll see what happens tomorrow when I show up at his office to collect the police reports and photographs. I told the sheriff that he had it all wrong again."

"He won't listen to you, you know."

"I hoped he might entertain the thought that he needs another suspect if Rube isn't the one."

"If Ballard runs true to form, he'll spend more time bad mouthing you and building his imaginary case then looking for someone new."

"I wouldn't think it would be too hard to find other people of interest. It seems to me that the murderer had to know about that operation. It's too far out of the way to be a random chance event. The farm has been in operation for many years. There probably have been dozens of kids run through there. Then there are probably more dozens of service people such as petroleum deliveries, vets, cream pickup people, repairmen and the list goes on."

"Have you heard any speculation around town?"

Tanner wrinkled his nose. "No. The sheriff and the DA blab so much at the Elks Club that everyone in town thinks they're privy to the inside story. If Rube would go to trial, he'd probably be convicted as soon as he walked into the courthouse. The jury pool has really been tainted."

Protecting his hand with a towel, Tanner lifted the lid off a large cast iron pot, dragging a puff of fragrant smoke with it. He slipped a large filet of salmon onto a plate. From another pot came a generous portion of roasted garlic mashed potatoes and from the refrigerator, a bowl of red cabbage slaw.

"Ummm," said Usher as he tasted the fish. "How'd you smoke this?"

"Line a heavy pot with foil. Dump in a couple of tablespoons of brown rice, brown sugar and the contents of a couple of bags of Earl Grey tea. Put your fish or chicken, scallops or whatever on a vegetable steamer."

"I'll remember that when I can't get to the roof BBQ unit in the winter."

CHAPTER 8

In the morning, Usher walked into the sheriff's office precisely at 10 am. He was expecting another run-in with Ballard but the sheriff wasn't there.

The matron asked Usher for identification and his letter of authorization before sliding a thin folder across the counter. Apparently, the DA had given the sheriff the word.

On the way into town, Usher had spotted a small diner with a practically bare parking lot. He was between the breakfast and lunch trade. The coffee was left over from the morning rush. In a back booth, Usher started through a folder. He found the reports were in chronological order. Marco Pali...that would have been Thumper...called the sheriff's office to report the murders.

As Usher read through the reports, he could see how Rube had become the primary suspect. The other seven kids had ironclad alibis at the school and on the bus. Rube was described as being an antisocial misfit and he had not gone into the school and then he disappeared.

Usher learned that Rube's fingerprints were all over the weapon and the room where Elizabeth Hardy had been found. She had been seated at her desk with her back toward the door. She'd been hit with a home run lefty swing. There had also been numerous other impacts.

Ed had been slugged as he left his improvised bedroom in the barn. This assailant had been standing in the stairwell going up to the hay mow. He got his left arm up and had it crushed. The killing blow was administered directly to the top of the head. Ed's crotch and genitals were obliterated.

Carefully, Usher went through the whole report and dallied over the crime scene photographs. Also included were photos of the kid's living areas with particular emphasis on Rube's room.

Usher returned the report to its folder, glanced at his watch and wondered if Freda Myers might be at her office. He asked the waitress for the location of the county social service offices.

Being such a small town, Usher could have walked. After some static from the receptionist, who wanted him to make an appointment for a later time, Usher was shown into a small, inglorious office.

Ms. Myers smiled, "How can I help you Mr. Orlop? The receptionist said you were making inquiries into the Hardy murders...a dreadful thing."

Yes, I'm the investigator for the office of HHC and H, attorneys at law. Here is a letter of authorization. Mr. Huuskonen represents Topi Mannisenimäki, also known as Rube."

"Oh dear, I've already talked to Topi's attorney.

"This is a change of attorneys. The reason I'm here is to

try to find the current location of Marco Pali. His nickname is Thumper.

""I'm sorry Mr. Orlop, we cannot divulge private information on our kids.

"Ms. Myers, we don't think Rube killed those people. Our main objective is to keep him from coming to trial because if he does there will be testimony that will curl your hair and fry this department. In fact it would be a good idea to get your supervisor in here, so he or she has some lead time to protect your jobs."

"Are you threatening us?"

"No. I'm just going to give you some very good reasons to help me find an alternative suspect"

"So far you haven't given me anything which would warrant bothering Mrs. Walker."

"Okay. Try this on for size. Did you know that Rube had precocious sexual development?"

"His medical records made reference to it."

"Well, the afternoon you dropped him off, Mrs. Hardy discovered the condition when she stripped him down while trying to fit him in work clothes. After making that discovery, every Thursday night from there on out Rube had the late dinner cleanup. During the cleanup, Mrs. Hardy retired to her downstairs office and sex solon where she would bathe and get ready for an evening of sex. If she got horny on Saturday night, she called Thumper to send Rube over. Oh, she liked it slow and deep."

"Oh, I don't believe this."

"It won't be hard to prove. All the kids knew what happening. And this is only the tip of the sexcapades. Do you wish to get Mrs. Walker now? Without a word, the very worried caseworker darted out of the office.

Usher had to wait some time. Mrs. Walker led the way into the office. Her job description did not call for a public smiley-face. This was a stern administrator.

"Mr. Orlop, what is all this flak that you're giving Ms. Myers?"

"I suppose Ms. Myers has already told you about Rube and Mrs. Hardy. Incidentally, have you ever met Mr. Hardy?"

The question was directed to Ms. Myers. She thought for a moment. "No, he was always out working."

"The reason was that there was no "Mr." Hardy. The Eds were just hired hands to run the ranch.

"What I'm about to tell you is not known to law enforcement and if Rube doesn't go to trial, this will never come up. But if Rube does have to go to court, his attorney will drag all of this out in excruciating detail." Usher proceeded to lay out the various sexual activities of the whole pack.

Ms. Myers sat in a state of worried shock. Her boss was already working on crisis control.

"I get your point Mr. Orlop. You're correct in assuming we would rather that this situation not come to light. What is it that you seek?"

"As I told Ms. Myers, I don't believe the Rube did this, so I'm looking for an alternative suspect. I believe that the murder had a direct connection with the farm. Since all the other kids have alibis, it could be anyone from the mailman to the feed and seed delivery man or even a former inmate of the farm. The best source of any information on anything would be Thumper, Marco Pali. All I'm asking for at this time is help in finding him."

Ms. Myers looked to her boss for guidance. She received an affirmative nod. "When this tragic event happened, Marco was just weeks from being released from our program. We would never have found a foster home for him. He was always a difficult one to place because of his attitude, so we discharged him."

"What does that mean? You sent him out to fend for himself. Did you provide him with transition money, food and lodging?"

"Mr. Usher," said Mrs. Walker. "This county has little money for this department and that doesn't extend to cash grants. All the kids are counseled to save their money and prepare their clothes and property to transit to the outside world when their time comes."

"I suppose the ranch was a good spot to make those preparations...money flowed freely and there were neighbor's lawns to mow."

"Many kids volunteer for the military. It is usually an easy transition."

"Did Thumper join the military?"

"No," said a very embarrassed Ms. Myers. "We received an inquiry from the Multnomah Sheriff's Office. He was being held on a burglary charge."

"Oh boy. What kind of building?"

"A little corner grocery store."

"I suppose they found him sitting on the corner stuffing his face."

"They don't provide type that of information," said an offended supervisor.

"I'm sorry. That was uncalled for. Do you suppose he is still there?"

"Probably," said the slightly miffed Mrs. Walker. He has no money or anyone to make bail for him. He'd be too much of a risk for a bail bondsman."

Usher moved to the front of his chair preparatory to rising. "Thank you ladies. We're actually on the same team. We don't want Rube to have to face these charges." Usher slid a business card across the desk. These are my home contacts and for the next few days you can reach me through this local phone number.

"Incidentally, watch out for Sheriff Ballard. My name will really set him off. I'm interfering with his reelection plans. If he finds out I was here, he'll be all over this place like a crime scene trying to find out what I wanted."

After taking leave of the social services office, Usher headed for Tanner's. He had to let himself in because his friend was off on a frolic of his own. That was all right because he had considerable planning to do. The large boiled-coffee pot was on the back of a trash burner, holding the contents at a drinkable temperature.

Usher spread the photos of the crime scene across the kitchen table. He'd liked to have gone to the farm, but he'd have to do battle with the sheriff again. To get a better idea of the scene, he googled the address for an aerial map.

After seeing the lay of the land, he was even more convinced the murderer had to be a former inmate. Since there are no alien tire tracks in the yard, the assailant would probably have parked in a gravel bus turnaround as a sheriff suspected Rube had done.

There was a fringe of intervening brush cutting off a view of the bus stop. The assailant would have had to wend his way around to the dormitory building for the aluminum bat. It certainly wouldn't have been a random weapon of opportunity. Intimate knowledge of the layout would have been needed to navigate around the farm yard without running the chance of being observed by either MB or Ed.

Of course, all of the prerequisites he was laying out would

have been met by Rube. It was becoming more obvious, that Thumper was his best source of contemporary information. If he didn't pan out, Usher would have to squeeze Mrs. Walker for records.

After checking in with Anasette, Usher prevailed on Rube's attorney to set up an interview with Thumper, who was indeed still in the Multnomah County Jail.

CHAPTER 9

At 11 am, Mr. Huuskonen was signing them in for a prisoner interview. They were directed to a small room furnished with a table and three chairs. The back wall was half glass with a door.

The two visitors had just seated themselves when a big, burly deputy herded a slightly built, swarthy youth through the door from the holding area. Usher had never bothered to formulate any image of Thumper, but he would have recognized the kid anywhere. At first glance, Usher began to laugh. It was not a polite, petite laugh, but a full blown gut-roller.

Thumper stopped in the doorway to the meeting room. The deputy prodded him forward enough to close the door.

Usher battled for control. Huuskonen wore a confused look. As the laughter subsided, Usher said, "Do you eat peas?"

Thumper curled his lip again."Nah, can't stand'em."

That set Usher off again."

Thumper was getting angry. "What's he laughing about?" demanded the kid of the attorney.

Huuskonen shrugged.

"Thumper, you have a talented understudy," said Usher. "In fact, he's ambidextrous. Rube can curl either side.

"I'm not going to talk to that laughing jackass," as he turned to have the deputy let him out.

"Thumper, I didn't come here to listen. I came here to talk. And it's definitely to your advantage to listen. Sit down and lend me your ear."

Thumper was close to acting contrary to Usher's suggestion, but his sharply honed self-preservation instincts went onto autopilot. He slouched down into his chair.

"My name is Usher Orlop. I am a friend of Topi Mannisenimäki, Rube. This is Mr. Huuskonen, Rube's attorney.

"Why are you talking to me?" interrupted Thumper. Us kids didn't have anything to do with those murders. We were in school."

"We don't think Rube had anything to do with them either. It is our intention to keep Rube from having to go on trial.

"Right now you're being held on a pissy-ass burglary charge. No matter which way it goes, it won't make much difference to the general scheme of your life. But if Rube goes to trial there will be all sorts of testimony on things that no official even knows exists."

Thumper probably would have placed his feet on the table if he thought he could get away with it. The sneer never left his face.

"Let me give you an example of the type of inquiry that Mr.

Huuskonen will be introducing in court. He might start out with the Thursday evenings when Rube stayed late after kitchen clean-up to service Mother Bear,

That jolted part of the sneer off Thumper's face.

"And then there were the Saturday evening when Mother Bear got horney and had you send Rube over for another romp. Of course everyone on the ranch knew what was going on.

"Then there was the situation with Raven. You may have had a door on your bedroom, but the walls are tissue thin. Of course, having a door didn't much difference when you parade naked in the shower afterwards...and entertain the boys with a blow-job.

"Of course, Raven just turned seventeen so there were months of sexual activity while she was below the age of consent. I'm not sure what they call it in this state. It's something like statutory rape or contributing to the delinquency of a minor.

"Then there was the procuring of Chip, Willie and Gin for Ed's favors. For these duties you received spending money, cigarettes and beer, which make you a pimp.

The sneer was replaced by an expression of concern.

"When the judge hears all this, I'd be willing to bet he'll remand you to the custody of the sheriff to be held for moral turpitude charges. And if you can ever get out of prison, you'll be branded a sexual predator, which means you must register with the police when you find a place to live. The police will warn all the neighbors that a pervert just moved in next door. In turn, the neighbors will scream 'Not in my neighborhood,' and drive you out so the whole process can start again."

"I get your point, Mr. Orlop. What do you want of me?"

"It is our contention that none of you kids did it, but it had to be someone who was intimately familiar with the operation. You were around there the longest. Do you remember any of the other kids who bore a big enough grudge to return and take such a violent action?"

"Naw, I've thought about that, but I can't think of anyone who'd do that. None of the kids liked MB or Ed but most of them didn't like other foster homes where they had stayed, either. I don't know any who would have had the guts to do it.

"How about service people? Suppliers?"

"MB was tight with her money, but not bad enough to get whacked."

"Give me a list of all the people you can recall that came frequently to the ranch." Mr. Huuskonen handed Usher a legal pad. It didn't take long because not many visited the ranch on a regular basis.

"Thumper," said Usher as he was wrapping up. "Who used the right-hand mitt that's hanging with the mitts in the athletic area?"

"The only lefty I can remember was Windy, which was short for Windmill. She was a hot-shot left-handed softball pitcher. No one around there could hit her. When she turned 18, the better part of a year ago, she could hardly wait to enlist in the army. She wanted to ride that left arm on to fame and fortune. She was not college material. She thought she could showcase her talents in the army."

"Did she make it?" said Usher.

"Never heard. Of course, that's a long-term building process."

"Well, Thumper, give Mr. Huuskonen a call if you think of something or hear something that will help keep this affair out of court. It would be to your advantage as well as Rube's."

On the way out of jail, Usher said, "Thanks Mr. Huuskonen for setting this up. I'd never have been able to see him privately on my own."

The attorney was smiling broadly. "What touched your funny bone when that ill-mannered little twerp was brought in?"

"When I first ran into Rube, he had that same curled lip snarl and the woman who took him in for a couple of days said, 'Oh he's only playacting.' Then at dinner Rube carefully picked through a dish to separate out all of the peas. As soon as I spotted Thumper, I knew that Carlee was right."

"Mr. Orlop, this is been an interesting morning. I must return to the office. Mr. Jangala is awaiting my call. I'm to give him a blow-by-blow account of the proceedings."

"I didn't think he'd taken any personal interest in the case."

"I think his main interest at this time is you."

"Me?"

"Your name surfaced during the affair with his grandson. Subsequent encounters have raised his curiosity. You must remember that Mr. Jangala used to be a mover and shaker. He has now passed on his power. His body has become a traitor, while his mind has stayed acute. Apparently, you seem to be able to give some degree of meaning to his day."

Usher shrugged. "I hope this interest continues until we can resolve Topi's problem."

"Jangala usually stays in the game until the bitter end."

"Good. I'll take these names back to Tillamook. Tanner may have some insight. If not he has the resources to make queries."

CHAPTER 10

When Usher drove into the compound behind the house, Tanner waved him over to one of the outbuildings.

"How'd your interview go?"

"You never did see a demonstration of Rube's sneer. Anasette wouldn't tolerate it. I found the prototype for the whole thing, including the repulsion to peas. When Thumper was brought in, I couldn't quit laughing." Usher perched on the end of the table as he gave Tanner a full account of the meeting with Thumper.

"Where do you go from here?"

"I only have one nickname of a girl who turned 18 about a year ago. She was a hotshot left-handed softball pitcher, who went into the army. I'll get her full name from Ms. Myers and check with the army. Where is the recruiting office?"

"There is little cubbyhole in the courthouse. All the services share the space. Each has an assigned date. I'll check when the army is in town."

"Here is a list of names and businesses who had reason to be on the ranch on a periodic basis. Would you look it over and see if you can spot any murderers in there."

"I'm about finished in here for the day. I'll look at it over a cup of coffee."

"What are you doing?"

"I'm holding my breath that this box is big enough to hold 100 pounds of garnets. I have an order from a dealer."

"Garnets?"

"Last summer, a friend told me of a new road excavation in Alaska that had exposed a large deposit of top grade garnets. I rented a truck from a friend and brought back quite a load. Many of them look as if they may star. The word has gotten out and I'm getting a good run on them."

The evening was spent on the phones and Internet. Usher checked in with Anasette, who required a blow-by-blow account of the events. He also reported to Jangala, who said he'd bring the attorney up to date.

Tanner found out that the army recruiter would be in the next day. He also began a round of calls getting background information on service personnel Thumper had identified.

In the morning, Usher caught Ms. Myers in the office before she went out on rounds. There was no hesitancy in giving out Windy's real name...Grace Welch. The social worker presumed Grace had gone directly into the army.

A large sandwich board directed Usher to the proper cubbyhole in the courthouse. The sign on the desk matched the name tag...Olsen.

"Sergeant Olsen, my name is Usher Orlop. I am trying to locate a young lady named Grace Welch. About 10 months ago she was released from a foster care program after graduation from high school, so she could enlist in the army. Do you have any record of that enlistment? I need to track her down."

"That would be before I was assigned here. Let me check the records. I can't divulge any personal information but I can give when and where she went."

The sergeant swiveled around to a filing cabinet with an army decal. It took some time and a considerable amount of muttering before he swung back to his desk.

"As far as I can tell, she didn't enlist here. She came in to enlist, but she didn't pass our physical. She was pregnant. The notes from the enlisting officer indicated she was really surprised and pissed off. Apparently Welch was going to get an abortion and be back, as soon as she felt all right. Either she changed her mind or enlisted elsewhere."

"Um, that throws a whole new complexion on the affair. Thank you, Sergeant."

Out in the parking lot, Usher mulled the new information around. The obvious plan of action was to find out if Windy had a abortion. There shouldn't be many abortionists in an area of low population.

Usher called Tanner's house. The answering machine picked up his call. All Usher said was, "I need some information. I'm heading back in." As Usher came out of the dense Oregon coastal brush through which Tanner's entry road passed, his mind was jerked away from his Windy speculation. A marked Sheriff's office patrol car sat in the parking lot in front of Tanner's fantastic forest. Crime scene tape stretched from one end of the compound to the other.

Tanner's old Army deuce and a half truck was parked on the roadside outside of the closed gate to the compound.

Ushers immediate concern was for Tanner's well-being. If his friend had a physical problem and had to call 911 there shouldn't have been crime scene tape

A deputy opened the driver's door of the patrol car, indicating his presence. As Usher neared, a young deputy stood up and put on his uniform cap.

Keeping his hands in sight, Usher got out of his car. "What's going on?"

"Police business. Who are you?"

I'm a houseguest of Tanner Jones. Where is he?"

The sheriff has taken him in for questioning."

"Questioning for what?"

"That's not your concern," said the young deputy with an arrogant flip of his head.

Usher was thinking of his notes and notations on the police report that was in Tanner' s house. His laptop was there with an extensive Rube file. He didn't want Ballard to even get a glimpse of that information.

"All my stuff's in there. I want to get it out."

"No one goes in there. The sheriff is going for a search warrant.

Usher could see he wasn't going to get anywhere with that pup. "Where did they take Tanner."

"It doesn't make any difference to you. You can't see him."

"I just want to know where to send his attorney."

"Humph," said the deputy as he climbed back into his car and picked up the radio mike.

Usher backed around into the parking lot that Tanner had

to put up to handle all the tourists who came to see the great steel arch that stood over his drift tree forest.

Jangala's number was in memory. The old man must've been up and about because he was on the phone shortly.

"Mr. Jangala, I ran into a hitch in the form of Ballard, the sheriff, who is trying to ride Topi into a reelection. I've had a run-in with him in the past. I'm no friend of his. He knows I'm messing around in his sandbox and it would appear that he is using his office to find out what I'm up to. He knows I always stay with Tanner. A moment ago I returned to the house and found Tanner has been taken in for questioning on something. His house is taped off as if it were a crime scene and guarded by a deputy. All of my notes and records on Topi are in there."

"Yeah, I know who Ballard is. His services and loyalties are for sale. What would you want of me?"

"Tanner will probably need outside legal representation and we need to block a search warrant. For years, Ballard has been trying to get into Tanners compound to snoop around."

"I'll call Huuskonen. Where can we get in touch with you?"

You have my cell number and I'm going to make contact with Tanner's sister, Tawny. Just a moment and I can get her number." He pulled her home phone number out of memory and gave it to Jangala.

After concluding with Jangala, Usher called Tawny. "This is Usher. I'm at Tanner's and there is a deputy parked out here and crime scene tape around the compound. Ballard has taken Tanner in for questioning. His deputy won't tell me why. Ballard is getting a search warrant."

Tawny, who is much more voluble than her brother,

exploded. "That damned bunch of gossiping old farts."

"Whoa, what are you talking about?"

"The Elks Club. That's where all the old boys meet and get drunk."

"What do they have to do with Tanner?"

"We have a friend, who is a bartender there. Ben has been warning Tanner that that bunch of lushes has been building a hypothetical case that Tanner is shipping drugs."

"Tawny, I'd better get out of here before Ballard tries to have me grabbed. That deputy is on the radio again. I'm coming over. Try to find out what you can. You can tell me the whole story when I get there."

Usher didn't like the way the deputy kept looking his way. This whole thing with Tanner was probably predicated on him injecting himself into the Ballard murder case. As soon as the patrol car door started to open, Usher started his car and swerved into the entry lane. The deputy jumped out of his car and tried to flag him down, but Usher didn't appear to look back.

The guard deputy probably couldn't leave his post, but that didn't preclude the sheriff from sending out another car.

Usher headed for the beach turnout where he first met Tanner. He could hide his car and still watch traffic on the coast highway.

He didn't have long to wait. Another car went by at high speed running under blue light. Usher let him get out of sight before heading north.

Knowing Usher's coffee addiction, Tawny had a fresh pot ready. The kids were at school.

"Have you found out anything," asked Usher"

"No one has heard a thing. I did find out that Ballard isn't at his office so he's probably at the jail building. They have interrogation rooms there."

I'm expecting a call from Jangala's attorney. While we're waiting, tell me about the Elks club thing."

"The Club here is the home territory of the old boy's network. More business is negotiated there then both at City Hall and the County Court House.

"Our bartender friend said that one night a post office worker said that Tanner was sending a lot of packages recently.. The owner of one of the Mail Box places said, "Yeah, he sending a lot of big, heavy crates too."

"Those guys have always been curious about how Tanner makes his money. Someone suggested he was a drug dealer. For weeks they have been building their fantasy case. Our friend warned Tanner that they were beginning to believe themselves."

"And Ballard is using this story to pickup Tanner?"

"I'd bet the farm on it."

Who are these guys at the club?"

"Oh, the mayor, male city council members, county commissioners, judges plus most of the prominent business men in town. All spend a lot of time there

"You say those buys drink a lot?"

"Sure do."

"Colorado has really been stomping down on drunk driving. Did Oregon get on the bandwagon?"

Sure. I belong to MADD and we lobbied for years to get the alcohol content down so that you'd watch out if you've have two beers.

How do the Elks make it home? Taxi's or designated driver?

"I told you that this was the good-ol-boys network. They reset the police shift change from midnight to 2:00 am. It's all arranged that the first night officers come in at1:00 am to write reports. At 2:00 am the late shift comes in. It takes them half an hour to get out the door. So there is an hour and a half window for the lushes to make their way home.

"The sheriff is part of the Elk's cadre. He doesn't want his men to poach in the city and they know not to arrest. It's mess.

Usher's phone rang. It was Huuskonen, saying that he'd been on the phone to the courthouse advising them that papers were in route to challenge the search warrant. The clerk seemed quite upset. I suspect he's being pressured by the other side. I've also called the sheriff's office to advise they are not to interview my client, Tanner Jones, without me or my representative present."

"Am I still your representative?'

"Ha," said Huuskonen with a laugh. That would be a bit of a stretch. Theoretically, you'd be there to render legal advice, which wouldn't work."

"Can I be assigned to guard your client's property?"

"The sheriff can walk right through you if he gets a search warrant."

"This isn't designed to keep him out but to irritate him and bring his actions to public attention.

Don't forget he can trump up charges on you as well as on Tanner.

"I'll call if anything changes."

Turning back to Tawny. Usher said, "How active is MADD

around here?"

"We have an active group, but it is difficult to change anything because this is an old time hard drinking area."

"Do you have time to show me the Elks Club?"

"Sure, let me turn down the heat under the sauce and get a coat."

"The club owns half a city block. The back quarter is overgrown with coastal brush. The front faces on one of the main streets in town. Its parking lot is on corner side of the building with entry and exits on both the street in front and the side street.

"When they arrive sober," said Tawny, "they go in the front door. But when they're drunk, they slip out the back door and staggger around to their cars and drive out the side exit."

"What kind of activity would you suspect tonight?"

"Oh, it'll be heavy. This is twofer night and I imagine word of Tanner being picked up will bring them by the droves."

Usher made the circuit of the block a couple more times. "Do you suppose MADD could round up four members who would be willing to stake out the place from, say 10:00 to 2:00?"

Tawny got a wicked smile on her face. "Easily. What do you need?"

Two non-descript cars...preferably with tinted windows. There should be a cell phone in each car for security purposes. Writing material and watches are all that's needed. Oh, yes binoculars might be handy.

"Do you have the number of Harold, the wildlife photographer?"

"At home. He's working out of his house.. He should be

home."

Usher took Twany home and stayed long enough to call tahe photographer to set up a shooting session.

"I'm going to head back to Tanner's. If they haven't released him yet, I'm going to set up a guard post in front of the gate into the compound. You might get on the phone and call Tanner's friends, asking them to fill up the parking lot and take pictures of the tape and forest. The local newspaper might even send their own photographer down. If you hear from Tanner, let me know."

Usher delayed long enough to pick up a couple of foot long subs, some bottled water and an enormous thermos cup of coffee before heading for Tanner's.

The same young deputy was still parked in front of the fantasy forest, close to the gigantic iron arch. Usher drove briskly past Tanner's old army truck to the locked gate into the compound. The deputy bailed out of his car. By the time the kid got there, Usher had turned around and placed his rear bumper just shy of the yellow tape across the gate.

"What are you doing here?" demanded the deputy.

"I've been instructed by Mr. Jones's attorney to guard his property against thievery."

"This is a crime scene."

"What crime?" sneered Usher, rolling his lip like Rube. "Besides I'm outside your crime tape."

The deputy apparently couldn't think of anything to say and besides, he should be reporting the latest developments. While the deputy talked at length on the radio, Usher unwrapped a toasted sub to begin lunch. He figured he'd get that out of the way before the sheriff arrived.

Twenty minutes later, the sheriff's car came busting out

of the entry lane. It came to a skidding halt without much room between the bumpers. Ballard had to vault over the bumpers by using the hoods of the cars.

"What are you doing here? This is a crime scene."

"If there was any crime scene, it would be behind the tape. I'm outside the tape."

"You're sticking your nose into something that doesn't concern you again," shouted the sheriff.

"Oh, but it is my concern. I represent Tanner's attorney and he says that I should protect Tanner's property.

How did that Portland shyster become Jone's attorney?"

Tanner is a friend of Yrlo Jangala. You are beginning to give the Little Tyrant an itch. It's not a good idea to do that. He might scratch."

Ballard was beyond critical thought. "I should run you in too. You know what's going on in this place."

"Do you really want to compound your original error of acting on a fabricated story by a bunch busy-body Elks?"

"That was too serious an allegation to ignore," protested the sheriff in self-defense. We can't have that sort of thing going on in the community. It's up to me to get to the bottom of this."

"Sheriff, if you want to get at me, Come at me directly. Don't go after my friends. When are you going to release Tanner?"

"He's not going anywhere until I get some answers and tomorrow morning there will be a hearing on my search warrant. Are you the one who screwed up my search warrant? Someone is filing an injunction, so now we have to have a hearing. Until then, no one get into that.... that....that...." The sheriff ended up just flipping a hand at

Tanner's compound. "No one is going to have a chance to destroy any evidence. You go by that tape and I'll have the deputy arrest you."

Ballard stomped around his car to get to the driver's door. He backed over to the other patrol car and worked the young deputy's ear a long time before jamming his car into drive and spinning his wheels toward the exit lane.

He didn't make it. The first of a long line of cars was occupying the one-way road. A caravan of about twenty cars and pickups filed into the parking area in front of the massive arch. Women and pre-school kids came boiling out of the cars. Most of the women had digital cameras or video cameras. Others just had their cell phones. The sheriff fled.

Usher picked up the second sub and a bottle of water. He headed for the entrapped patrol car. "Looks as if you're going to be around here awhile. I bought two of these, thinking I would be here a lot longer. I'm leaving, so enjoy...and I won't tell the sheriff." He was aware that cameras were going off all around him.

Settling down in a remote booth in a diner, Usher began making his phone calls. The first on his list was Anasette. "Sheriff Ballard is trying to screw things up. Doesn't dare come at me directly so he picked up Tanner on a trumped up charge."

"What? Tanner?'

"I wouldn't worry about him. He may not be able to leave, I'll bet that when the cat's away, he has the whole department sitting around drinking coffee and swapping stories.

Usher gave an abbreviated account of the happenings. "I'll have to cut this off until I can get to a landline or I can get my charger from Tanner's. I'll call you later."

Next, Usher bludgeoned his way through an iron-pants house-mother to talk with Rube.

"Hi Rube. Just checking to see that you haven't wandered off again."

"Hi Mr. Orlop. You told me to stay put. Have you found out anything yet?

"We have a list of names of people who know the layout at the ranch. We're working our way through it. Hang in there. My phone is about out of juice. I'll talk to you later."

Usher sat back. That had been a hard call. Rube's voice was dripping with fear. Something had to be done and done soon.

Not wanting to try making any more calls until he got a charge, he headed for Tawny's.

"Any word on Tanner?" said Tawny as Usher let himself in the back door.

"Ballard is still holding him. Apparently, Huuskonen stop the judge from issuing a search warrant until there could be a hearing tomorrow. If everything goes well, we'll have Tanner out in the morning and be rid of this foolishness. I'm going to have to get back to Denver and this is wasting my time.

"Tawny," said Usher, "you'd probably be better able to answer this than your brother. If a girl wants an abortion, where would she go?"

"Here in Tillamook?"

"Yes."

"There is a part-time clinic in an old house just north of town. They're open a couple of days a week. You can't miss the place. There are always protesters heckling the doctors and the women.

"Is the clinic open today?"

"I can find out." Tawny made two calls before reporting, "You're in luck. They are open today."

"Good. I'll drop by there first, then I'll buy some toiletries and find a motel."

"I'm sure Misha would gladly trade his bed for the couch if you'd stay here. Both boys would be delighted to see you."

"Thanks, but I don't want the sheriff to connect your family and Misha with me. That's why Tanner is being held. Besides, it should be a busy night. Are the mothers set up?"

"Oh boy, are they. I had several more volunteer calls. They even have permission from two homeowners for the use of their driveways so girls won't have to park on the street."

Usher held up his cell phone. "Do you know where I can get a charger for this?"

"That outfit has an outlet on the main street."

As Usher passed through town, he picked up an auto charger for his phone. Then he headed north. Tawny had been right. The clinic was very obvious with all the "baby killer" sandwich boards. There were three women and a pimply faced youth standing on the sidewalk. They converged on Usher's car as he turned toward the small parking lot beside the house.

"Don't go in there. They're baby killers." The boy took up a position on blocking Usher from entering, while the women shouted invectives.

Usher shifted into park, relaxed in the seat and put an amused expression on his face. The women shouted themselves out and eventually they came to the conclusion that they were just a source of entertainment. Usher cracked a window to ask, "Do I look as if I need an abortion?" One of the women waved the male off to the side so Usher could park by the only other car in the lot.

The former living room had been converted into a waiting room. The dining room was now an office dominated by a large desk back by filing cabinets. The double sliding doors were open. The woman sitting behind the desk looked up from her sudoku puzzle as Usher walked in.

"May I help you?"

"I hope so. I'm Usher Orlop, an investigator for an attorney who is trying to locate a young woman who is wanted as a witness in court."

The woman broke in. "We can't divulge any information concerning our clients."

"Wait, wait. Let me finish. About 10 months ago, an 18-year-old girl tried to enlist in the army. She found that she was pregnant. Apparently, it was her intention to get an abortion and return to the recruiter. This never happened. We don't know if she changed her mind about the abortion or if she enlisted elsewhere. There was a very powerful motivation to join the army."

"I told you, I can't tell you if this girl was treated here."

"Could you tell me if she didn't get an abortion?"

The woman rolled her eyes toward the ceiling. "Who was this girl?"

"Grace Welch."

"I handle all the paperwork here and I don't recognize that name."

"Grace was just coming out of years of foster care. She had no money or any family backing. If she didn't come here, where could she go to have the procedure performed?"

"There is another clinic in Astoria, or it would probably be easier to hop a bus for Portland."

"I'd hoped I might get lucky. I was figuring that because of her financial circumstances and the time element that she'd beat a path to your door."

"She might have intended to come here, but occasionally those Bible thumpers outside snag a girl. They are experts in laying a guilt trip on the women who come here."

Thanks for your help."

On the way back to his car, Usher suddenly change directions and headed for the protesters.

"I hear that every once in a while you guys are able to show one of the potential customers here the error of their intentions."

"Yes," said the woman who had been screaming at him a few minutes earlier. It is always a joy to save a precious baby. That's what keeps us here."

"I'm trying to locate a girl who was headed in there about nine or 10 months ago but apparently she didn't make it. I was wondering if she might have been one of your savings. Her name was Grace Welch."

"Don't recognize the name."

One of the other women had come up to join the conversation. "Sometimes, the girls don't use their real names."

"She is a tall, athletic girl with the nickname of Windy," said Usher.

"Wait," said the second woman. "That sounds as if it might be Millie's softball player."

"That sounds like the right one. How would I find out what happened to her?"

"We protect the privacy of our girls."

"I'm an investigator for an attorney who is interested in Grace as a witness in a court case.

"We can't say much anyway. We're not an organized group so there are no central records. Millie handled that girl and about two months ago Millie had a massive stroke. She's completely out of it."

"Too bad," said Usher. "I had hoped this would be a simple thing. Is there anything you can tell me?"

"No, not really. The girl is not here. Millie had a family in Astoria where she could stay until she had the baby. I know that the baby was to be adopted. The girl should have had the baby by now and she'd be out on her own."

Before Usher headed for the drugstore, he wrote down Millie's name and address just in case a relative or friend might have access to Millie's papers.

Later, he found a motel with inadequate lounge and restaurant. Using his room phone to call Anasette, he brought her up to date. He always paid a penalty when her curiosity wasn't promptly satiated.

"The whole business with the sheriff is slowing things down. I have to get back to Denver. There are some deadlines that have to be met.

"Rube?"

"He didn't sound good when I talked to him on the phone this afternoon. He's not far from panicing, which wouldn't be good."

"What can you do?"

"It's probably dinnertime at JDH. I'm going to get something to eat and then show up at the door to see if I can talk with him. I really had a battle to get to talk to him a bit this afternoon and I'm pretty sure somebody was listening in.

Usher would much rather have had razor clams, but they weren't on the menu. He settled for Dungeness crab in barbecue sauce. He passed on the martini because of the impending nocturnal activities.

After dinner, Usher headed for the juvenile detention facilities. The front office was closed so there was a prolonged wait until someone came up from the back. This time it was a male house parent.

"I'm Usher Orlop, the representative of Rube Mannisenimäki's attorney. I have some instructions for Rube from Mr. Huuskonen."

"The office is closed. You'll have to come back tomorrow."

"I need to relay some information to him. I tried to call earlier this afternoon. I talked with him briefly, but I'm sure somebody was listening to our conversation. Mr. Huuskonen would not like his instructions to become public knowledge, so I came to talk to him in person."

"I told you..."

Usher held a copy of the letter from the attorney against the glass in the door while he considered his argument. "This is a capital case. I don't want to cause anyone any trouble, but you can bet that Sheriff Ballard would not take kindly to anyone that could jeopardize his case. Coming between a client and his attorney could create a real problem."

The house parent lost some of his authoritarian bravado and wanted to read the letter again.

"Let me go to my car for my cell phone. I'll call Sheriff Ballard and have him come over to straighten things out."

That was obviously an unpopular suggestion. The house parent countered with, "I can call my supervisor."

"Is she the hard, precise woman I talked to earlier?"

"Probably."

"If she gets involved, I will have to call the sheriff. I've already done battle with her. I doubt if I rate too highly with her. Why don't we just make this easy and let me talk to the boy. I also want to calm him down. He sounded really scared when I talked with him earlier. We wouldn't want him to do anything foolish, would we? That could really screw things up."

"Okay, but you have to stay far enough away from him so you can't pass him anything."

"That's all right. Just so we can have a little conversational privacy.

The house parent led Usher through the staff area to a small dining room. There were four picnic benches. "You sit on that one and Rube can sit on the next one. I'll be watching through the glass in the kitchen door.

The man picked up the house phone "Gladys, please bring Rube to the dining room."

Usher stood by his appointed table, while the house parent repeated admonition, "Now don't pass him anything..."

The rasp of a key in the lock of the door between the dining room and the reception area interrupted the instructions. Gladys was a broad, matronly woman. Her girth filled the window in the door. When she pushed the door open and stepped into the room the house parent's interaction held Rube's attention. He didn't immediately notice Ushers standing off to the side.

Rube was dressed in jeans, a white T-shirt and sneakers. There was no role-playing...no expression of bored indifference or curled lip hostility. He didn't seem to have bones...just a lump of pail lard.

The man started to tell Rube, "You'll have to sit at this table..."

When Rube's attention shifted toward the table, he spotted Usher. He flashed across the intervening space, "Mr. Orlop" and grabbed Usher around the waist, burying his head in Ushers rib cage. Usher flashed his open palms to the house parents before returning the hug. He could feel the sobs shaking the tiny frame.

Usher let the sobs subside before he gently steered Rube to a bench. "The hardest thing in the whole world is to handle uncertainty, especially when you're personally involved." Usher slid into the other bench. Rube hung his head, apparently not wishing to display his tears.

Usher's mind was racing trying to figure out how to handle the situation. This was a long ways out of his comfort zone. He wasn't prepared for so much raw emotion. While trying to frame the words that he knew would not offer any hope, he collected Rube's small cold clammy hands in his.

"Rube, I want you to know what's happening and what to expect."

"Have you found out who did it, yet?"

"We're working on it, but nothing yet. Tanner is going to be eliminating various names that Thumper gave me. You have to remember you're involved in a long drawn out process. In this kind of thing involving courts and lawyers, everything is very slow."

"But Mr. Orlop, I've got to get out of here. Everyone so mean. The other kids are the worst."

"I'm afraid you're stuck here until we either find out who killed those people or the courts determine that you didn't. You'll have to do the best you can."

Whatever Rube had hoped to hear, that wasn't it. He

began quivering again and his expression nearly tore Usher apart.

"Rube, you don't have to try to impress anyone around here. When I was talking with Ms. Myers, she said you'd always been hard to place because you are unresponsive to anything. That was play acting just like Thumper's sneer, right?" There was a minute bob of the head.

"That worked for you once. Why not try again? Just ignore all those hateful kids and unkind adults. But let me give you a warning. Don't try that with Anasette. She'll hand you your head."

A hint of a smile flicked past his upper lip, as Rube began to rearrange his facial structure. The eyes hooded. The muscles around his mouth went slack. The head tilted a little to the right. When his eyes turned back to Usher, there was a completely different kid in front of him. Rube pulled his hands away and let them go slack and motionless on the table.

Usher shook his head. "Mrs. Brown said you were good. I have a couple of things I need to do but tomorrow or the next day, I have to return to Denver. There are some deadlines that I must meet.

"Tanner will be checking some possible leads. I'll drop off all the police reports with Mr. Huuskonen. He will be working his end of this."

With that news, Rubes mask almost broke but he regrouped and gave Usher an indifferent shrug.

"Not wanting to tell Rube about Tanner's current situation, Usher gave a couple of vague reasons he had to leave. The announcement was acknowledged with equally vague eyes.

Usher turned Rube over to Gladys and followed the male

house parent back to the front office.

"Don't be alarmed, Rube has shifted into a defensive mode to a handle spiteful comments."

"Of course," said the house parent. "Little is said around us, but we can read body language enough to know what's going on. It really must be tough on Rube."

"Does he have a Rubik's cube?"

"No. The kids can't have any personal things here."

"If I donate a cube to the home, do you suppose you could put it where Rube could find it?"

The house parent smiled. "Yeah. I think I could handle that."

CHAPTER 11

A check with Tawny and Harold found all to be in readiness. Tanner hadn't put in an appearance. Usher didn't know Oregon law, but he suspected that Tanner was being detained unlawfully, but when the sheriffs and the DAs jobs were at stake he wouldn't get far by pointing that out. Usher liked the prospects of his plan better.

It took three stops before Usher located a Rubik's cube. Then he settled down for a martini.

An early-morning check with Tawny revealed that Tanner was still missing. After a quick breakfast Usher met the MAAD night shift at Tawny's and picked up whatever he would need for his confrontation with Sheriff Ballard.

A check of the sheriff's private parking spot revealed the sheriff hadn't put in an appearance yet. When Usher entered the office there was only a matron behind the desk. Voices could be heard coming from the inner sanctum.

"May I help you?" said the matron as Usher approached the counter.

"I'm here to pick up Tanner Jones."

"Has the sheriff released him? I haven't been told yet."

"No, but he's about to. I'm running on a very tight schedule. So please call the sheriff and tell him that I, Usher Orlop, am here for Tanner Jones. If I don't walk out of here with Tanner in 30 minutes, even sacrificing a 12-year-old won't save his job.

The matron started to object but Usher interrupted. "If Ballard misses his deadline because you wanted to waste time arguing with me, I'd hate to be in your position. You don't want to share in his lumps."

Apparently the matron decided it wasn't in her job description to stage any dangerous defensive action for the sheriff. She thumbed the Mike and ran through the call signs. "There is an Usher Orlop in the office to pick up Mr. Jones. He says you have half an hour to comply."

"What? I'll be there in five minutes."

Everyone in the office noted the sheriffs impending arrival long before he put in a physical appearance from the squall the tires and the bottoming out of the patrol car as he hit the curb cut. There was a series of door slamming before he entered the rear of the office.

"Orlop," yelled Ballard. I told you to stay out of my business. What kind of crap are you shoveling now?"

Usher had been leaning casually against the counter. He straightened up and glanced at his wristwatch. Turning his attention to the enraged law enforcement officer, he said, "Sheriff, perhaps we should step in to your office. I rather doubt you want what I have to say to become local gossip."

Ballard inhaled deeply to render a thunderous reply, but suddenly thought better of it. He crossed swords with this pesky artist before and hadn't fared well. Besides, a civilian couple just entered the office. A deputy had come from the back to watch the proceedings.

Ballard wheeled around and led the way to his office. Usher shut the door behind himself.

"Okay, Let's have it" snarled the infuriating sheriff.

Usher handed Ballard a little video camera with the screen extended. "Push the button to see a little clip of a much longer film."

The sheriff pushed the button. At first he didn't recognize the image of a figure staggering out the door until the photographer zoomed in on the person.

"The mayor!" said Ballard in an appalled sounding voice. He continued to watch his honor stagger around the back corner of the Elks club into the parking lot where he climbed into his car and made his erratic way out the side entrance.

Usher reach for the camera with one hand as he handed the concerned sheriff a sheet of paper.

"Here's a list of 20 of your leading citizens including a County Commissioner and a circuit court judge. All of them are in the same condition and there are four MADD witnesses to each, plus the videos

Usher glanced at his watch again. "You only have 15 minutes."

"Until what?"

"Until a contingent of MADD members enter the city attorney's office to get warrants for DWIL on all 20. At the same time, another contingent leaves town for Salem to file a complaint with the Attorney General should the city attorney not comply by the time they get to the capital. This will all go into motion unless I call them off within the allotted time."

"And how do I prevent this and if I do, how do I know you won't do it anyway?"

"You have to released Tanner and remove that crime scene designation as well as drop this bogus investigation. MAAD will hold their material to make sure you don't start in on Tanner again as soon as I leave town. You'll have to trust them just as they'll have to trust you.

"Time is getting short. You better start moving Tanner in this direction."

Ballard picked up the phone, dialed the number and barked, "Bring Jones to the office fast... and I mean FAST."

"He is just across the street."

"Good," said Usher, as he glanced at his watch. "We better meet him at the front door because there is a watcher stationed to make sure we walk." Usher opened the door and as he passed through the office Usher said "Call your deputy to takedown that tape at Tanner's and vacate the property."

Without replying, the sheriff stopped by the radio and issued a terse order. He was so furious his voice cracked while using the radio, which raised his anger level even higher.

Usher began to wonder if Ballard would be able to maintain control. In an attempt to ease the pressure, Usher pointed out that the sheriff had no alternative. "If 20 of the most prominent citizens were arrested for DUIL because of one of your actions, they probably will tar and feather you or what ever the modern equivalent would be. They're not going to remember that their wild speculations are at fault."

By then, they were standing on the sidewalk to the front entry. Ballard was searching for the "watcher." He still wasn't talking.

Usher continued, "If this comes out, you better point out that you weren't photographed because you had a deputy pick you and the DA up and returned with another officer to collect your cars.

Ballard bobbed his head off to the right. Tanner was crossing the street at the intersection. As a parting shot, Usher said, "We won't use any of this unless you take any further actions against Tanner or me or any of the people who took part in this little operation...and you're still wrong about Rube."

Before Ballard could reply, Usher's stepped way to go meet Tanner. He wasn't sure what might happen if Tanner came up with his own usually insightful comments.

Tanner had a broad grin on his face as the two men met. Being in inveterate hand shaker, Tanner had his hand out.

"I suppose I have you to thank for this rescue. Thanks. I need something decent to eat."

"Let's get out of here before the sheriff loses it. He is on a very short fuse," said Usher as he led the way to his rental car that he had parked on the street.

Tanner turned to wave goodbye to the sheriff, but the furious one had already retreated to the office.

When Usher pulled out of sight of the office, he called Tawny. "I got him."

"Connie, the watcher, already called. I'll put the coffee on. Come tell me all about it."

To Tanner, Usher reported, "we're heading for your sister's house. She, MADD and your photographer friend Harold pulled whole thing off.

"I'm glad to be out of there, but it was an interesting experience. They never did charge me with anything, so I didn't get fingerprinted or booked into jail. They just kept me in a room where the deputies relax and eat their lunch. I'm sure Ballard does want to get into my house. But apparently he had to do it legally and something got in his way."

Both men held their stories during the short drive to Tawny's. Tanner found it hilarious on how he'd been broken out. Finally, Tanner said, "I have to get home. I need some real food. All they fed me was fast food hamburgers and tacos. The coffee was like tepid water.

On the way home, Tanner said, "Turn right. We'll stop by Dewey's for some Dungeness crab. It'll take a few minutes. I'll have Dewey steam them for us. That'll save some time.

Usher went in with Tanner. Living in the middle of the country, fish dinners seldom stared back at you unless you go to an Asian market.

As the two diners started to fill the container in the center of the table with empty crab shells, Tanner asked, "How's Rube?"

"He's a scared little boy, but I think he'll hold out, at least in the short term. I want to get him out of there. I think I have...how do they say it?... a person of interest.

"Grace Welch, Windy, the softball pitcher didn't make it into the army." Usher related what he knew. She may have enlisted after having the baby. I'll try to find out from the army. Huuskonen should know how to go about that. If not, can you try to pick up her trail in Astoria?"

"Sure," said Tanner as he began moving the debris from the table. The coffee was bubbling away. "I can go up there tomorrow. There should be some hospital records, birth certificates."

"As far as I can see, there is little that I can do right now. I will go to Portland tomorrow, report to Jangala and hand over the police reports and whatever I have to the attorney. And I'll head back for Denver. I have some things there that need attention.

"I'll take care of Astoria and if that doesn't pan out, I'll go over that list that Thumper gave you."

"Say, I bought a Rubik's cube. I'm going to donate it to JDH since Rube can't have any personal property. Could you drop it off in the evening to the male house parent? They'll see that Rube gets it."

CHAPTER 12

When Usher finally made it back to Denver, Anasette was waiting to pick him up. That way she'd have an extended period of time to get a blow-by-blow account of the happenings during the long drive into the city. She had developed a fondness for Rube.

Usher never minded discussing matters with Anasette. Her creative mind usually found nuggets he blundered over. He tended to dwell on variant patterns where she recognized details. Maybe that was a reflection of their work scale. Usher thought of sculpture as being life-sized, where anything larger than a scarab would have been too gross in Anasette's mind

As the Shelby took the freeway off ramp, Anasette said, "I didn't suspect you would be back so soon, so I don't have as much to eat in the place. You don't have anything either. We'll just have to stop at Fahrenheit 451."

In the dimly lighted car, Anasette had a smug look on her face. They'd be arriving after happy hour. The hors d'oeuvre table would be cleared away so Usher could not fill up on shrimp and all the other goodies. By then he loses his appetite and doesn't want to go into the dining room. Anasette wanted a filet mignon with all the sautéed mushrooms she could eat.

After dinner Usher headed for a studio. Anasette peeled off to change into her winter uniform. Usher made his habitual inspection of the studio. Upstairs, he stripped-down for a leisurely shower. While drying off, he flipped on the answering machine more to get rid of a winking red evil eye than to find out what disasters may have occurred. He came to an abrupt halt when the last message started.

"Mr. Orlop. This is Freda Myers from Tillamook human services. Would you call me as soon as possible. I have some information that may be important." She gave her office number and also her home phone number in case she had left the office.

Usher wrote the numbers on a scratch pad and finished dressing. The elevator descended for Anasette, who was to join him for a drink. When she arrived Usher shouted, "Set up at the bar so we can use the speakerphone. Something has happened in Tillamook."

When Usher finished dressing, he found Anasette had set out all the makings for a Black Russian and his martini. The phone was between their two stools.

"The social worker called to say she had something that might be important. The woman is very anxious that Rube never goes to court, so this information may or may not have value."

"Then you can mix my Black Russian first."

After serving the drinks, Usher checked his watch. It was probably too late to catch her at the office. He dialed the home number.

"Ms. Myers, this is Usher Orlop."

Oh, Mr. Orlop, I'm so glad you called. You are interested in one of our girls, Grace Welch. This afternoon I had a call from a Lieutenant Granger of the state police in Astoria. He was calling to get information on Grace. She was identified by fingerprints that were taken back when Grace came into our system.

"Is she dead?" said Usher.

"Yes, she was killed in an auto-train accident just outside of Astoria...on the same day as the other parties were killed. The lieutenant said it was a bloody accident with lots of damage to the body. I thought you'd like to know."

"You thought right. Thank you. Did the lieutenant give any more information as to how it happened?"

"No, he asked about her address and next of kin. All I could tell him was that Grace was an orphan with no known family. I couldn't give information about where she was living because I hadn't heard from her since she passed out of our control. She had planned on going into the army."

"Well, thank you Ms. Myers. Let's hope this helps Rube. If you hear anything more please either call me or Tanner Jones. Do you know Tanner?"

"Sure, I know him...everyone does."

After the connection was broken, Usher lapsed into thought. Anasette held her questions, knowing that Usher's mind would be racing.

Finally, he took a sip of his martini. And she questioned him by raising her eyebrows.

"My operating theory is that Grace had her baby and when she recovered, she came looking for the guy who knocked her up and interfered with her plans. I would suspect that that so-called accident was probably suicide, but that is not all of the story. She could have still gone into the army and gotten her pitching showcase."

"Are you going back to Oregon?"

"No, not now. Tanner can handle the accident much better than I can." Usher took Tanner's number out of the phone memory and hit the button.

"Hey, Tanner. I just returned a call from Ms. Myers, the social worker." Usher relayed the information he'd received. "Do you suppose you can get hold of your state police friend to see if he can get a copy of the accident report or anything else he can scrape up?"

I can probably find out more by going up there. I planned on being there tomorrow anyway."

"You might suggest that the police checked the blood on the body and clothes to see if it's all her's.

Anasette giggled when Tanner said, "That thought had crossed my mind too." She loved it when somebody matched Tanner's thought process. It kept him from getting too arrogant.

"Is that Anasette?"

"Hi Tanner. I hear you been doing bad things...ending up in jail."

Tanner laughed. "Yeah, horrid. I have a couple of star garnets, if you'd like them."

"Oh yes, and I'll promise not to mention jail anymore."

"I'll send them to you. Incidentally, did you get that little package I sent to you?"

"Oops," said Anasette as she jumped down from her stool and dashed to the elevator with her white bathrobe flowing behind her.

"What was that?" said Tanner.

"I'd say that Anasette accepted the package while I was gone and forgot to mention it."

Quickly the elevator was returning. Anasette held a small wrapped package about 4 inches square. "Sorry. Open it!"

Both males had a laugh that Anasette's open display of eager curiosity.

After Usher slit open the wrapping and distributed Styrofoam packing across the countertop, he was rewarded with a red silk wrapper. Inside was a tiny Brazilian bloodstone carving of a rope knot. It was only 2.5 inches long and an inch wide and half an inch high.

There was an audible intake of breath from Anasette. "It's gorgeous."

Usher said, "Boy, that kid is getting good."

"It's a reef knot...two ropes tied together. Look closely at the compression of the ropes. He put tension on the knot."

"Where did he come up with the idea?" said Anasette.

"I was sawing long slices from a piece of that bloodstone I bought that time Misha and I sorted through a ton of new material. When Misha saw the first cut, he got excited and asked for the round end piece. How that kid saw something so clearly in a chunk of rock is a mystery.

"Anyway, he wants to make something for you. The tied ropes have some sort of symbolism for him."

"I'll call him right away," said Usher. "This will hold a special place in my gallery."

Before he hung up, Tanner assured Usher that he take care of Astoria and whatever else had to be done. He'd report any progress the next evening.

****

Usher's schedule for the next day called for the making of the mold of Rube's sculpture but Usher was too jittery for the precise nature of the work. He thought about taking it to a mold maker. He mentally tabulated the additional expenses you'd be running up against the fee he was collecting from Jangala. He also had to deduct his Oregon expenses. He'd hoped to be able to cast an artist's proof at the same time, but if he took the plasteline to a mold-maker there wouldn't be enough money unless he dug into his own pocket.

Apparently, Anasette was having similar concentration problems. She risked Usher's displeasure if she interrupted any critical work. When she noted the lack of any progress, she smiled as she said, "Coffee?"

The coffee break lasted until lunch. Finally, Usher decided to go to his office to work on the books. Later, Anasette joined him for a meal of whatever they could find. They still hadn't gone grocery shopping. The agony continued on through dinner and into the evening because of the time differences.

When the telephone finally rang, both artists jump. Usher took the call on the speakerphone.

"Hi Tanner, Anasette is here with me. How'd you do?"

"We have our murderer. All I have to do is convince the various authorities. Incidentally, Ballard doesn't know yet. I want to be around when he finds out.

"Come on, let's hear it," said Anasette.

"After dark on the day that the Hardys were killed, Grace Welch wedged the front end of her car under a boxcar at a rural crossing. The car was dragged a long ways down the track. There wasn't much left. Ms. Myers was right. It was a bloody mess. There was so much bodily damage no one thought about checking the blood. I made the suggestion that they check the type of blood on the shoes and clothes. When I suggested they might be able to clear a double murder they suddenly became more interested in paying for some lab work.

"Grace was not carrying any identification. The car proved to be a dead end. She had bought it off the street from a kid only the day before. She paid $150.

"They took what prints that were left and sent them off to the FBI. That is how they got back to human services.

"While they were checking the blood, I went to the hospital to see what I could find out about the baby. I ran into a brick wall trying to get around their privacy policy."

"How do you beat that?" said Anasette.

"There was a large board that had photos of the whole staff. I recognize an old classmate of mine. She wasn't on duty, but I called her at home. We had a nice little chat. When she found out what I needed, she wouldn't give me any medical history, but she did tell me the names of the doctors."

"Doctors?" said Usher. "Do you need 'doctors' to have a baby?"

"Something went wrong and Grace was in the hospital for five days."

"What happened? said Anasette.

"They wouldn't tell me. So I went back to the state police office. By then the blood had been typed. There were two or more... at least A and O. There could've been multiple As or Os, but that would take more time.

"With that information, Lieutenant Mankowski opened up and told me the various particulars. Grace was in a T-shirt, jeans and sneakers. There was also a sweatshirt in the car area.

"She had a wad of bills stuffed in her left rear pocket. There are some small receipts...the tear out kind from a little pad. There were dates, amounts and names such as Ed, Thumper."

"Aha!" yelled Usher.

"Apparently, MB made little receipts when she handed out cash. When the meaning of the receipts became evident the lieutenant knew we had the right person. He and I went back to the hospital and found out most of what we needed to know. The official documents will have to go through the proper legal channels.

"Anyway the story is that as a result of the pregnancy and the subsequent birth, she had a small hypertension stroke on the right side of the brain, which slightly impaired the movement of her left side. Most observers would probably never notice any problem, but apparently Grace went all to pieces when the doctor told her what was wrong. She could no longer pitch."

Tanner paused. The silence dragged on for some time before he resumed. His voice changed tone. "From what I understand, pitching was Grace's is one chance for a future. Just think of the fantasies an orphan/foster child would have built at such a prospect. The stroke would have kept her out of the military too."

"Oh," said Anasette, "that poor girl. 'Ed'." The name came out sounding like a growl.

Usher offered the observation, "The only one that got what she wanted was the anti-abortion woman, Millie, at the cost of three lives and weeks of terror for a little boy"

Tanner brought the group back to order by saying, "Tomorrow Lieutenant `Mankowski and I are going to go to the DAs office for a release for Rube. If the DA doesn't call Ballard over, we'll look him up to make him release Rube."

"That's great," said Usher, with passion.

"You know, tomorrow I'll have a 12-year-old on my hands. I'll have to turn him back over to Ms. Myers.

"Do you suppose you could put him at Tawny's for the night. I have an idea, but I haven't tried to set up anything until I know Rube will be released."

"Yeah, I think it can be arranged, but it can't be a permanent thing. We can't draw any attention to Misha's situation.

"I better get busy on the phone," said Usher. "Great work. Let us know if anything changes."

After Usher broke the connection, Anasette turned to him with an expectant expression. When the Usher didn't immediately begin a narrative, she said "Well?"

"I have some thinking to do first."

Anasette knew that Usher wouldn't talk until he had mentally constructed a skeleton upon which to hang a course of action. Even though she knew that this was the case, it still didn't set well. She hopped off her stool, gathered her robe around her and march to the elevator without looking back.

Usher was a little miffed that Anasette took that attitude. Under normal conditions he would have expected that would happen, but this time he had figured she'd have stuck around long enough for a celebratory drink to Rube's impending release.

It was well into the night before Usher had what he wanted. He went to bed with a smile on his face. Things were falling into line and he had also received some help on Rube's expenses so in the morning he could take his plasteline figure to the mold maker.

In the morning, as soon as Usher started to move about the kitchen to get his morning coffee the elevator started up. Apparently, Anasette had been waiting for the squeak of the ancient wooden floors. She couldn't maintain her miff without losing much more, so she ignored the whole situation as if it had never taken place.

Usher set out another cup and then launched into a quick disclosure of his evening activities. He wanted to get back from the mold maker early enough that he would not miss Tanner's call.

Again it was a nervous wait. Finally, the call came at two o'clock.

"I have him," announced Tanner in his big, booming voice. "I just dropped in at my sister's place. I thought it would be better to make this call without an audience."

"Congratulations," said Usher and Anasette added her "Good work."

"What happened when you went to pick him up?"

"Lieutenant Mankowski made an early trip from Astoria. He and I caught the DA just as he reached his office. We were standing in the outer office, within earshot of the coffee pot. It was choice. The lieutenant introduced himself and said, "I believe you know Mr. Jones. We have identified the murderer of Mrs. Hardy and Ed. And it's not the kid, Topi Mannisenimäki, who you're holding. We've come for a release for the boy. Here's a copy of the preliminary reports."

"Stanley's mouth dropped open, but nothing came out until the second try. It only took him that long to throw Sheriff Ballard to the army ants. He started to cover his whatcha-call-it."

"Ass," injected Anasette.

Tanner gave a little uncomfortable grunt because he would never have used the exact term in mixed company.

"Yes, anyway, he went into a long explanation of how Ballard had issued all sorts of assurances that he had the right person. Stanley told a secretary to get the sheriff over there pronto.

While we are waiting for the sheriff, the DA scans through the report. Mankowski pointed out the salient points such as the blood types and money and receipts. The DA was a believer by the time the sheriff arrived."

Usher asked, "What did Ballard have to say?"

"When he saw me there, he had to stifle an instant surge of anger. Stanley quickly pulled Ballard into his office. The walls must be soundproof because only the loudest shouts penetrated as muffled cries. There was a lot of that going on.

"Finally, the secretary was summoned. When she returned she made a call to JDH ordering them to release Rube to me as a representative of attorney Huuskonen. Official papers were to follow as well as report to human services."

"You mean it was that easy?" said Anassette.

"I guess they decided it would be in their best interests to get Rube out of custody as soon as possible once they were aware of his innocence. Remember the election is only a short time away and there is the possible liability of false imprisonment. And," chuckled Tanner, "there are still the Elks Club photos somewhere. They might be able to weather a botched investigation but not if they were to have the whole upper crust of the local social structure on their backs too."

"Was Rube glad to see you?" said Usher.

"At first he thought the sheriff was just playing a trick to get him to talk. It wasn't until he was brought out to the waiting room and he saw me that he permitted himself to believe what the house parents were telling them. He couldn't get out of that door fast enough. It wasn't until he locked himself in my car that he relaxed enough to ask what happened."

"I can't even imagine," said Anasette, "what a burden was lifted off of him to find he wasn't looking at the possibility of spending virtually his whole life in prison."

"We went directly to Tawny's so I could just give him the short form version of all that transpired. What do you want to do with him?"

"In the morning, would you be able to take him to Portland to give his thanks to Mr. Jangala, who made all this possible? After that, airmail him to me. I'll reimburse you for your expenses."

"What are you ultimately going to do with him?"

"He has some important decisions to make. This is something that he must decide." Usher proceeded to give Tanner a brief description of Rube's choices. Call me with his arrival time. I'll let you know which way things go."

Again it was a hard wait. Neither Usher nor Anasette were able to concentrate so they both ended up doing housecleaning. Usher had a lady come in once a week to keep the gallery clean as well as areas where invitees might be expected to go. Usher handled the rest.

It was just after 6 pm when Usher and Anasette joined the throngs of people awaiting the new arrivals outside of the security area. Rube wasn't easy to find in a compacted crowd. Finally, Anasette spotted him. He was wearing his "I don't give a shit" mask.

He disappeared again into the surging humanity. The next time he popped into view, Anasette stuck an arm in the air and waved.

When Rube spotted Usher and Anasette, the mask fell. It was replaced by the biggest grin his little face could hold. He bolted through the crowd ending up with an arm around each artist and his face buried between them so that one touched each cheek.

After some inane questions such as, "How was your flight? How are you? Glad to see you again," eventually everyone regained enough composure to move off. Automatically, Usher began to head for the baggage claims, until he realized Rube carried all of his worldly possessions on his body or in his virtually empty backpack.

After Usher paid the ransom money as Shelby Mustang, he prompted Rube to tell about his release from JDH and his meeting with Jangala.

"I thought they were playing with me again," said Rube. "The sheriff had wanted me to walk them through the murder scene. Everyone knew I did it. They kept figuring I was too dumb to realize that they had goods on me. They couldn't figure out why I wouldn't cooperate and maybe make it easier on myself.

I couldn't figure out why one of the house parents slipped me the Rubik's cube until I figured out it was you who had sent it to me. Thanks, that made things a lot easier. Then when we went to the front office and Mr. Jones was there, I didn't know what to expect.

"When we got in the car, he told me about the girl, Grace."

Rube fielded a bunch of questions from Anasette to satisfy her curiosity.

"How did you get along with Mr. Jangala?" said Usher.

"He wasn't as scary this time. He already knew almost everything that had happened. He asked about little things... about how I felt about various things, what I dreamed about, how did I like the food where I was, what I thought about the human services people...things like that.

"One funny thing..."

"Mr. Jangala was at his desk when we walked in. He tossed me a mixed up Rubik cube and said fix it.

"My payback for all his help was a promise to write a letter to him once a week. It is supposed to be hand written—not an e-mail. It can't be 'I'm fine, how are you?' He wants to know what I do, what I learned and how I feel about things"

"Do you plan on keeping your promise?"

"You bet."

"You know, that won't be easy. There will be all sorts of things that keep getting in your way. The only possibility of you keeping your promise is to decide that the letter is a priority in your life. It must come first, before any distractions.

Rube didn't say anything.

Usher was keeping an eye on Rube in the rearview mirror. Anasette had turned sideways in her seat. In the dim light of a strangled day, they watched a series of thoughts play across the youngster's face. This was something new. He was being asked to make a decision that could affect his own future.

After a prolonged silence, Rube grinned his crooked little grin and said, "Yeah, I can do that."

There was another pause. Then Rube said, "Is that one of

the decisions I would have to make? Mr. Jangala told me I was coming to see you and you would tell me what choices I have."

"No, That wasn't what Mr. Jangala had in mind. That was just an example of a lot of alternatives you will face as you get older. One of the major choices we all have to make is whether or not our word is going to be worth anything. Years ago when Anasette and I were somewhere around your age, we both decided to make our words sacred. I don't make many promises because if I do, I will move mountains to keep my word.

"What Mr. Jangala had in mind has to wait until you get back to the studio. First you have another thank you visit to make."

"Where?"

Anasette stepped in, "Let me tell him. You always leave out too much. When Tanner called to tell us you were wanted for a double murder, Usher immediately said they were looking for the wrong person, but he knew the situation must run its course. Both of us were feeling lousy, so we went to Maruca's Mexican restaurant. She is a dear friend and if anyone can cheer us up it would be her. She's the one who told Usher that if he didn't think you'd killed those two people then he should find out who did. So Usher's involvement was a direct result of Maruca's logic. We are going there for dinner. Hope you can eat Mexican food. You would not want to insult Maruca.

"I like tacos. Does that count?"

"It's a good start," said Anasette with a laugh.

"Mis Amigos! shouted Maruca across the restaurant and over the customer's heads. As she moved to greet them, she spotted Rube. "Aye. Is this our young murderer?"

Rube ducked his head and blushed furiously.

Usher bobbed his head.

Maruca scooped Rube into her ample bosom to give him a great hug. "Welcome, Usher told me you didn't do it. Since you're here, he must have proven it. Come, come, you must tell me all about it."

Since Usher & Co. had been spotted, Maruca had been throwing her usual arm signals to the staff. By the time the parties made it to the round booth in the back corner by the kitchen, it had been cleared of paper mats and napkins, wrapped flatware and replaced with a bright Mexican tablecloth, napkins and ornate flatware. Juan, Maraca's husband, stuck his head out of the kitchen to see what all the fuss was about. When he saw Usher and Anasette, he waved and smiled brightly before ducking back inside.

Maruca supervised seating. She showed Rube around the circular table to the back. Anasette and Usher were directed to the left, leaving the right side next to Rube for herself. If Juan joined them, he'd pull up a chair.

Usher and Anasette were known by the staff, so fresh coffee was on the way. One of the girls asked what Rube drank. There was too much accent for him to understand so Usher supplied, Café con Leche.

Seldom do the artists have to order because Maruca was going to serve them the best the house had to offer. On this occasion, it was huachinango. Speaking to Rube, Maruca said, "Tonight you will taste how Mexicans turn a lowly fish into a cena magnifica.

As soon as all the chores were completed, the Maruca slid up against Rube and said, "Now, tell me the whole story." Rube didn't know where to start so Usher had him describe the farm and the people. As the story progressed either Usher or Anasette filled in those portions that Rube didn't know about. This was the first time he'd heard much of what it happened while he was sitting in JDH. He was getting wrapped up in his own story. Anasette broke in whenever Usher skipped over his own exploits.

The story flowed through the meal with only a couple of interruptions such as when Rube chomped into too hot a chilly. Periodically, Juan joined them to hear bits of the story.

As the story finally wound down, coffee spiked with Kahlúa was served. Maruca slid her mug over to Rube for a sip. In response to the looks she received, she said, "A guy has to learn about the world where he lives."

While Usher and Anasette were bundling up against the cold, Maruca gave Rube a warm, prolonged hug. "If you ever come up with one of these you don't know what to do with, I'll take care of it." Maruca was smiling, but a tear escaped. Anasette immediately gave her a quizzical look. "The sad side of my former profession."

Anasette gave their hostess a hug before stepping out into the first flakes of a new snowfall. "What was that all about?" said Usher.

"Apparently, Maruca is sterile."

"Ugh," said Usher.

When the trio arrived at the studio, Usher said, "How about some of your herbal tea? I think we're probably coffeed out."

Anasette stopped in her apartment while Usher and Rube went ahead to heat the water. Anasette arranged the seating so that Rube was directly across the dining bar from Usher.

"Decision time," said Usher. I only have two choices, but the choice will be yours. Both choices have obligations, which you'll have to be willing to meet before they become viable choices.

Rube was looking bleak.

Anasette leaned over to grip the boy's hand. "Don't let Usher get to you. He has a tendency to dramatize everything."

Usher shook his head. "Okay, here's the deal. When you were here before, we went over the situation where you can't make it alone at your age. The first proposition is for you to go back into the system in Tillamook for the next six years. You already know the system and you can survive until you are able to strike out on your own.

"The other choice takes a longer commitment on your part. Remember the lady in Albuquerque, Carlee Brown..."

Rube's face fell. He looked back and forth between Usher and Anasette in desperation.

Anasette was off her stool in a flash to hug the distressed boy.

"Oh Rube, I'm sorry I set up the wrong impression by being so mysterious," said Usher.. It's not possible for you to live with us. In this state the authorities would never permit it. Both of us are single and the social workers would find a long list of reasons why they can't put a young boy under our control.

"When Tanner said you would be released, I started calling around trying to set up an alternative to you going back into the Tillamook system.

This is what I was able to find. You know that Mrs. Brown has a bunch of problems. She has a back problem. Also her ex-husband is always playing games with her support money.

"Anyway, when I got word you needed new accommodations, I called Mr. Jangala. And whether you know it or not, he still has a protective feeling toward River Finns. I don't know if you have a specific heritage, but being a Finn was enough for him.

"Mr. Jangala has more money than he'll ever spend, so I threw out the proposition that he invest in your future and help a couple of others at the same time. He agreed if I could set up the other end.

"I called Mrs. Brown with the proposition that if she were to open up her home to you, Mr. Jangala would provide enough money to take care of your expenses and additional funds to cover household expenses so that she wouldn't have to beg her lousy ex-husband.

"The current plan is to remodel the unused portion of a garage into a bedroom and bath for you. You will have a major say in design, color, furnishings and decor. You'd get a new school wardrobe and enroll in the appropriate grade.

"To choose this route needs a firm commitment from you to make it work. You have to do your part. You have to become a contributing member of the family." Usher paused for a moment. "And don't forget your picking up a little sister. You've met Lindee."

A smile crept across Rube face.

"No more curled lip snarls or passive detachment," injected Anasette.

"We are asking you for your answer in the morning." said Usher. "If you decide to go to Albuquerque, we'll leave early the next day. That's Saturday, so Lindee will be at home. If you choose to go to Tillamook, we'll make reservations.

"Anasette and I have some things to do. Go into the gallery to think or look around." Rube slid off his stool and refilled his cup, from the hot pot before disappearing around the corner.

Anasette looked questioningly at Usher who switched on the "Miraculous Mandarin" before answering. "There never was any question about where he'd go, but I wanted him to make that commitment to make it work."

The two artists were going over household matters and trip plans when "Mr. Usher," floated in from the gallery. When Usher answered, Rube came around the corner. "What's that little green thing in the glass case?"

"That's a reef knot carved out of bloodstone by Misha who you met at Tawny's."

"Misha? He's just a kid."

"What's wrong with that? Kids can do great things too."

"Ya, but..."

"Look at you and the cube," said Anasette.

"Ya, but..."

"There's no 'Ya, buts, about it," said Usher "If you commit yourself to a task, you can do it. Misha decided to sit at his made over treadle sewing machine for as many dozens of hours as it took to carve that little treasure. He has a couple things going for him. He has the ability to visualize all of those interlocking shapes and a dedication to see a project through. Other than that there is nothing special about Misha. You met him."

"I don't think he likes me."

"Probably still miffed that you snitched his 'creative shirt'."

"Creative shirt?"

"He wears a special shirt when he's creating something."

"Is that knot in the gallery for sale?"

"No," said Anasette. "Misha made that as a very special thank you for Usher."

Rube's big eyes swung back to Usher.

"Aw," said Usher with a dismissive wave of the hand. "Come with me, Rube. We'll bring up a cot for you to sleep on tonight."

"Oh, I don't mind sleeping in the studio. I kind of like it down there."

"Suit yourself."

"Come down with me," said Anasette, as she slid off her stool. "I'll get you a robe. She put her arm around Rube as they headed for the elevator. She shot "See ya in the morning," back to Usher.

CHAPTER 13

When Usher took the elevator down to get Rube for breakfast, he found the youngster in the white robe and grey socks asleep on the top of the packing crate where he had sat while watching Usher sculpt his likeness not that long ago. His clothes had been tossed on the made-up cot. He never made it to bed.

As the oversized elevator doors shut, the air pressure changed and the substantial thump roused Rube. He investigated the studio through drowsy eyes. He gave a stiff shrug before he found Usher leaning against the wall with a grin on his face.

"I'll have to remember that pose. It may find its way into another sculpture. Ready for breakfast?"

Rube bobbed his head. "I can do it, Mr. Orlop. I can make it work."

"Make what work?"

"I can make living at Mrs. Brown's work. I thought about it all night. I've been in so many foster homes, but I always figured I'd just represented a welfare check at the beginning of each month. To me, social workers were like mechanical toys. Someone wound them up every day so they could jump around from 8 to 5.

"Now I have real people trying to help me. I have to make it work."

"Once you come to a decision, the hard part is done. Come on, if we let Anasette's omelets get cold we will be wearing it as soon as we step out of the elevator."

****

The Shelby Mustang backed out of the parking slot well before dawn. It was an uneventful drive to Albuquerque. Rube didn't add much to the conversation. Facing a major life change was making him apprehensive.

The front window curtains fluttered as Usher opened the driver's door. The motion was quickly followed by a plainly audible shriek, "Mom, they're here."

Anasette laughed, "Have you ever had a little sister?"

"None like that."

"You are in for an interesting experience."

Rube didn't question that comment. He covered himself by making a play of collecting his backpack that contained his few worldly possessions.

Lindee opened the door as soon as the visitors touched the front porch. Carlee welcomed them in. Usher introduced Anasette and turned to Rube. "May I present master Topi Mannisenimäki, more commonly known as Rube."

Lindee rolled "Topi" around on her tongue, while the owner

of the name waited for her to rhyme it, which never came.

"Topi. I like it," declared Lindee. "That's better than having a brother called Dick."

"The coffee is ready, said Carlee. She had heated milk for Rube's café con leche and hot water for Lindee's tea.

As soon as all were served, Carlee turned to the two kids who she'd seated behind a table, against the window. "There's a bit of housekeeping that needs attention." To Rube she said, "I've never thought it to be good form for kids to call their parents by their first names. I'm experienced in answering to Mother or Mom but not Ma. Can you handle that?"

Rube bobbed his head.

"Try it out" she coached, "Mom."

Rue produced a rather awkward "Mom."

"Good, it'll get easier with time. Now, this is my house and I'm boss. I make the big decisions around here. That doesn't mean that I won't listen to your thoughts, but if you can't convince me to the contrary, my decision is law. Can you handle that?"

Rube rolled big puppy eyes up to look at Carlee. However, the seriousness of the occasion was compromised by an impish little smile at the corners of his mouth. He said "Yes, mother."

Lindee squealed with glee at the little inner game. "I'm going to have fun with a big brother. I can threaten all the big bullies at my school that I'll have my big brother make mock mince meat out of them."

"Hey, I'm not very big either."

"We'll be at different schools and they'll never know. Besides, you'll wow them with the Rubik's cube.

Carlee broke into the exchange. "Rube you'll have to sleep with the animals until we can get your room built."

"I can sleep on the cot in the studio."

"Unless I'm firing the kiln, it's too cold. You'll have to use the studio bathroom. There is a little heater to take the chill off."

"Oh, that reminds me. Usher, I have another wall plaque for you to look at."

"Great. The other doorway is pouting so much I can hardly get through it.."

When the coffee cups were drained, Usher said, "Anasette and I are going to check into that motel where we dropped off the freeway."

"Oh, I thought you'd have dinner with us." said Carlee

"You guys have a lot of arrangements to make. We'll buy you breakfast tomorrow morning at nine o'clock at Waffle House next to the motel."

"Waffles," said Rube in such a wistful tone he attracted everyone's attention.

"Do you think they have berry syrup?"

Carlee smiled, "I'm sure they do. Whenever you want waffles just pull the waffle iron from the cupboard under the oven. Lindee can show you how to make the batter. She is an expert on crepes too."

"What are crepes?"

"They are really yummy," declared Lindee. They're like little thin pancakes. I like them rolled up with apricot jam and powdered sugar over the top."

"Let's see the plaque," said Usher as he stood. The whole group trooped into the living room. After appreciative utterances and purchase negotiations, Usher gave the Mustang keys to Anasette to open the car as he carried his new acquisition out.

****

"None of the foster homes that I was in ever made waffles," said Rube as a defense against his second order of Belgian waffles."

"Enjoy it while you can," said Carlee. There will be days when we eat chicken, but there may well be days when we have to eat the shadow."

As the breakfast progressed, Lindee was able to brag on the writing award she just won. In turn each reported on a current creative project. As the focus moved around the table, Anasette was keeping her eye on Rube, who was left out of the conversation. He was becoming uncomfortable with his inability to participate. He was gradually slipping into his indifferent defensive mode.

Anasette picked a lull. "Carlee did you ever solve the problem of the warps of the Faerie house roofs?"

Carlee made a sour face. "I've given up on them. Everybody loves them, but my breakage rate is too high to make it profitable."

"I think Rube may have solved your problem."

Rube snapped back to the conversation with the mention of his name, but he'd missed the first part of the exchange.

Anasette pulled a shiny copper object from her purse. It was about 3 x 8" in size and slightly curved. "How would your houses look with copper shakes?"

"They'd be spectacular,"

"Eeeeeee," cried Lindee.

Carlee fingered the copper shake replicas. "If you can make

a roof like this, I'll turn the whole Faerie house thing over to you. There should be a good market for them."

Rube looked around the horn trying to determine if they were teasing him.

With an excited trill, Lindee said, "Where'd you learn to do that?"

Struggling with control and an impish smirk, Rube said, "Oh, it's just one of those prison trades they teach you."

Lindee threw an ineffectual punch at Rube's shoulder.

On that note, Usher and Anasette took their leave. Their last glimpse of the new family was Carlee standing in the parking lot with her arms around both kids' shoulders. The kids were waving goodbye.

Epilogue

Tanner called the day after the election saying that both Ballard and Stanley races were too close to call. There was going to be a recount. A couple of weeks later the report was that both had lost.

In early January, Tanner called while Usher and Anasette were finishing off a bottle of wine they opened for dinner. They took the call at the dining bar because of the speakerphone.

After the preliminaries, Tanner reported "Jim Stanley just opened up a new law office in Tillamook and guess who will be his chief investigator?"

"Ha," said Usher "That will be a pair. Watch yourself. I don't think either of them like you."

Before Tanner rang off, he said "What do you hear from Rube?"

"We received a really nice hand written, formal thank you from him. I think Carlee probably had a hand in that."

After Tanner's call, Usher was refilling the glasses when Anasette said, "Let's give Carlee a call. The kids are probably in bed, but Carlee is the night owl."

"Hi Carlee, this is Usher. Anasette is on the speakerphone with me. Tanner just called and he asked about Rube so we thought we'd give you a jingle and ask the same question.

"There is a bump here and there, but everything is fine. Topi isn't used to having to make decisions. He knows what he likes and dislikes, but he's never had the opportunity to express an opinion. "The evening you guys left, we started designing his room. We measure the space, location of the windows, wiring, plumbing and all that stuff. I showed him how to make a scale drawing on graph paper. Then he had to design his room. Where do the doors go, lights and plug-ins? He had been measuring beds to see if they would fit. It was a real workout."

"How'd he do?" said Usher.

"With a little help, he did fine. I picked out the contractor and he did just as Topi laid it out. Then came decisions on carpet color, wall color, bedding etc. He came up with the darndest color scheme"

"What?" said Anasette.

"It's an off shade of blue, two creams and then odd red."

Usher began to laugh. "Those are the Finnish color from Lyyli's Linx Lair...her boat. How's it look?"

"I wouldn't have given you a plug nickel for all that paint, but after we got it up, it distinctly has an appeal. I'm looking at all my off-white walls with new disdain."

"Has he moved in yet?" said Usher.

"Not entirely. He's still sleeping with the animals. We ran into trouble with the furniture. We made the rounds and he kept vetoing the lines we could afford. I was about ready to force a decision, when he found the unfinished furniture store. We're waiting for the paint to dry completely before he moves in permanently.

"He's a surprisingly frugal shopper. I thought he would go wild when we went out clothes shopping. He didn'i want any of those mod things that kids can't live without. He has a good eye for fashion. Oh, you'd laugh. There was some extra money in the clothes budget. I took him to a Western outfitters where, at my insistence, he bought himself a Pendleton shirt. He picked a blue plaid. It's hard to believe how proud he is of that shirt. He paraded around the house with the little price tag dangling from the collar. He was sneaking to my room to see himself in my three-way mirror.

When he finally had to take the tag off to wear it to school, he made over an old army surplus ammo box that my ex had left around. In the junk drawer, he found a couple of hinges, a hasp and a combination lock. He made a lockbox for his treasures. It's painted his room colors. The first thing to go into the box was the tag off of his Pendleton shirt."

"What do you think about him having a lockbox?" said Usher.

"It was cute. He must've figured I might object, so he asked permission and gave me the combination with a promise he would never put anything bad in it.

"He has a real thing for boxes. We were driving down an alley when he spotted a wooden packing crate. He just had to have it. He went inside and got permission to take it. We had a heck-of-a-time getting it wedged into the van along with all the clay supplies we were carrying. It must be 3' x 2' x 18". Topi sanded and fussed over that box before painting it. The box sits before the front window and that is his 'thinking box'."

"Hah," said Usher. "I'll bet that comes from the packing crate in my studio. He spent hours sitting on it watching me sculpt his likeness. Then the night that he had to make a decision about joining you, he spent the whole night on that crate."

"The other day I was making clay slabs for one of my projects. Topi asked for some clay. He made a box about the size of his cube. There was a hole torn in one side revealing an eye looking out at you. He sent that to Mr. Jangala."

"How's he doing on his letter writing to Mr. Jangala?" said Usher.

"He's placed a high priority on that obligation. When he finishes with his afterschool snack, he writes a paragraph about the most important events of his day. It can be anything from a blog he saw or the results of a science experiment. Every Monday, the letter goes into the mail. "Mr. Jangala responds to each letter. He has Topi trying out various handwriting styles. I think he will gravitate to Jangala's very distinctive style but with a little more flourish."

"Has he done anything with the Faerie house project?" said Anasette.

"Oh boy. We cut the warped roof off the house that I was going to junk. He fashioned a roof frame from heavy welding rod. A friend of mine welded it together. Topi is showing great dedication to a very slow, labor-intensive project. He cuts every copper shake for a specific spot. I suggested he make three tabs like asphalt roofing. He wouldn't hear of it. That roof is shaping up to be a magnificent piece."

"It sounds as if he might have a winner in a niche market," said Usher. "It should command a good price."

"This one is not for sale. It's to be a very special thank you gift. Don't you dare let him know you're aware of it. He's intensely proud of what he's doing."

"You bet I won't. It sounds as if Rube is discovering his creative identity and the copper shakes will be his coming-out party."

"How's Lindee dealing with a big brother?" said Anasette.

"She's having a great time keeping Topi off balance. She

can be pesty on one hand and then uncomfortably direct on the other. A few nights ago I was watching TV when Lindee's screeched "Mom, you gotta see this!" I bolted for the studio and found Topi pinned to the wall and Lindee trying to snatch his bath towel away.

Lindee knows about boys. She and my sister's son have been tossed into the tub together ever since they were old enough not to drown. I told Lindee to quit. I knew all about it. Right after Topi arrived, I took him to the pediatrician. It was a bit of a traumatic experience to have a female doctor. The three of us sat down and the doctor explained that boys are always teased about the size of their feet and their penises but they usually grow into them. Topi will always be well endowed but not as much as now. He still has some growing to do.

"I think that little foray in the studio was premeditated. You know Lindee has never seen a door she didn't slam. And yet she made it through the kitchen door and the studio door without a sound."

Everyone had a good laugh.

"It's nice to have Topi around the house. He is a big help. He doesn't want me to lift anything. He's very protective of both Lindee and me. In Mexico it is believed that if you want a dedicated watchdog, bringing in a street dog.

"Or a pound puppy," said Usher.

ISBN 978-0-9820044-4-9